The Unbroken Bond

To my friend, Kathy
Barbara McGaw
Gladen

The Warmth of Love in the Cold of the Alaskan Iditarod

The Unbroken Bond

Barbara McGaw Gladen

World of Fiction Publishing

The Unbroken Bond: The Warmth of Love in the Cold of the Alaskan Iditarod

World of Fiction Publishing

Published by
World of Fiction Publishing
An Imprint of Harmon Press
Woodinville, WA 98077
http://www.harmonpress.com

ISBN-10: 0-9799076-4-0
ISBN-13: 978-0-9799076-4-7

Library of Congress Control Number: 2008942662

Contents

ACKNOWLEDGEMENTS

To: My very dear grandson, Eric. You were very helpful. You gathered facts for me about early Alaska that I was not aware of when I started my story. I couldn't have done it without you.

IN MEMORIAM

Marian McGaw Herrmann (Mimi)
1931-2007

I want to thank my sister, Mimi, who always encouraged me to "Go For It." When you look down from heaven, you will see me "Going For It." I will always love you. Thank you so much!

THE UNBROKEN BOND

PART ONE

A TRAGEDY IN FORT YUKON

PROLOGUE

She was awake!

Her senses told her it was windy, stormy, and the thunder hurt her ears with its roar. The wind rattled the small window. She glanced over to make sure the glass wasn't broken. The rain was a solid patter on the roof. A sharp pain hit her!

She couldn't breathe for a moment. She sat up and looked around. She realized she was in a hospital bed with a bright light hanging overhead. She saw her clothes crumpled on a chair across from her.

The pain was coming again! Oh, God! Why is it so hard?

She screamed! Why was it so hard to breathe?

Her mind couldn't fathom what was happening to her.

She heard more screaming!

It was from her—the screaming was from her!

Oh, the pain! It seemed forever!

Finally, there was someone holding her hand. A voice was telling her to push down and breathe. She pushed down. Several times! Then, suddenly, she felt the pain go away. A small cry filled her ears. Of course, a baby! She just had a baby! She sighed. So tired! She lay quiet, moving slightly on the bed. A baby! Her eyes closed. She sighed again.

She was asleep.

Later that night, a thought came to her. She was awake, waiting for her dinner when it occurred to her that the nurse hadn't brought in her baby. She wondered whether it was a girl or boy? She really wanted to know. It was so quiet. Where was everyone?

The sound of trays came to her. The nurse brought in her tray and put it on her bed table. She sat up and smiled, "Where is my baby?" she asked sweetly. "When can I see it? Is it a boy? Is It a girl?" She waited for an answer as she took a bite of food.

The nurse looked at her curiously, saying nothing. Then she answered petulantly, "I don't know what you are talking about."

The nurse started out of the room.

She asked again, "Where is my baby?

Again the nurse answered angrily. "There isn't any baby here." She turned to the girl who was sitting in bed. "We have never had a baby delivered here. Where did you get that idea?"

She almost ran to the door and left.

The girl in the bed was stunned. She did not understand. What had happened?

As she lay there, eating a little, someone else came in and stood by her bed. She looked up.

It was the doctor. He smiled. "You are being very inquisitive, my dear. You are here for my treatment of appendicitis, not for having a baby." He grinned a funny little grin. He calmly told her that in the morning, she was free to go. Then he left, turning out the bright light. She lay back on her pillow and tried to remember how she got to this hospital.

The little red sports car was traveling at a very high speed. She didn't care. She just wanted to get away. The tears were coming fast and hard. She could hardly keep the car on the road. The pain in her stomach made her slow down. It made her think about what Gary had just told her. He had just told her he was going to marry Mary Lattimore!

She should have known! She was glad she never told him about the baby. She never told Joshua about it, either. She had found this little hospital on one of her drives. She had checked in when the pain was getting severe. The rain started as she was making the turn into the parking lot. It was almost dark.

She remembered walking in. Someone had undressed her and put her to bed. The bright light came on. She turned to see who was in the room. It was a nurse.

"Where is my baby?" She waited for an answer and waited and waited.

The nurse shook her head. She said angrily, "What baby? There's no baby here." She walked out. The bright light went out. The girl in the bed started to cry. Why were they lying? Finally she fell asleep.

Later the nurse looked in and saw that she was asleep. She thought with a shrug, at least, tonight will be a quiet one for a change. The rain seemed to prove her right. The storm was slowly moving off into the distance

The next day she awoke. It was painful, but she managed to put on her clothes. She saw her mink coat folded on the chair. She raised her hand to her neck. Her diamond necklace was still there. She picked up the mink and flung it over her shoulders. She waited for someone to come for her. No one did.

She walked out past the front desk. No one was there. She saw her red sports car parked where she had left it. She walked over to it and got in. The key was still in the ignition. That's odd, she thought. She really didn't care anymore. She turned it on and pulled out to the end of the driveway, turned toward town, and drove down the highway at breakneck speed. The rain had stopped, but the road was slippery. She didn't even think about it. Her foot went down on the pedal and the little red sports car sped down the road, her dark, curly hair flying. She shrugged off the mink coat and started to speed up faster. All of a sudden, the car lurched! She could feel the wheels sliding—so fast—she lost control.

She never saw the large tree in front of her!. She never heard the crash!

The rain started up, pelting her body relentlessly. The lightning flashed, the thunder just roared. When the policeman found her, she was slumped over the wheel. He pulled her gleaming, wet hair away from her face. He was stunned! She was so beautiful. He knew who she was. He was not sure how he would tell his captain about this horrific accident. He just kept standing there, staring at that beautiful face.

The rain kept pelting her motionless body.

CHAPTER 1

THE ARCTIC: DECEMBER 1968

The world was white on white as far as the eye could see. The horizon blended in with the sky until there was a nothingness. And cold! So cold her body was numb in her parka. It must have been forty below. But she was used to that. The sled just kept sliding along, racing against the wind and the sky. Her dogs were steady in their traces, glad to be running out again. Nefra, her lead dog, twitched her ears and laid them back when she heard the short, happy laugh. The two were one to another, they shared love forever. No one would understand unless they had gone through the pain that Nadia and Nefra had.

Nadia! "No," she thought to herself. "Not Nadia now."

She was Starflower now, and proud of it.

She shook her head, glancing up at the sky. It was beginning to darken. A snowstorm was just behind her. It could be less than an hour. She had to hurry! She had to get to Nome before the blizzard. She had to tell the people of the terrible flood in Fairbanks. She had to tell them of another tragedy, too.

Tears started to form in her beautiful dark eyes. She brushed them away. The flood had destroyed Fairbanks last April. Most of the villages were still in ruins. The streets of her village were still full of mud. Houses were gone. The swirling waters washed away many people. Whole families were wiped out. Those who survived came down with dysentery.

Some of them died. Starflower had lost her parents.

The good Doctor Luma took her in. She was just sixteen! She had helped him with his patients. Slowly she learned to like being a nurse. But five months later, the good doctor had contracted the disease and died. It had been a severe bout.

Nadia was, once again, alone. She blinked back the tears, remembering.

It took several months for the survivors to clean up the mud and debris from the streets. They were going to rebuild their town. They had sent Nadia to Fort Yukon to Charlie and Annie. She was too young to help in the rebuilding. She had learned some knowledge of the medical procedures that Doctor Luma had used and the townspeople knew that Charlie would help her to learn more.

The tears stung her eyes as she struggled with the sled. The snow was ankle deep over a tundra. The wind was coming stronger now. It blew one of her furs in the sled out onto the snow. She slowed the dogs to a walk. Nefra obeyed her command instantly. She ran back the few feet and grabbed it up. The dogs were getting too far ahead but she caught up and flung the fur onto the sled with the other furs as she pushed the dogs on. Nefra never faltered in her traces. She pulled Pookie, Pal, Nanuk, and Lucky steadily along with her. Starflower looked up at the sky. It was almost black now. The storm was moving in.

She didn't like to think about her father and mother or Charlie and Annie. They had been kind to her. They had taken her in and let her work in the little store Charlie had owned. All the people of Fort Yukon traded with him. In fact, even people from the Canadian Provinces came to see him. She loved to talk with them. They had so much to tell her about the world beyond Fort Yukon. Oh, how she had wanted to go with them!

Charlie had been a believer in school. "Book-larnnin," he had called it. She had loved going to school. Annie had made her a dress with pearly buttons and little ruffles. Everyone said she was pretty that first day. Charlie had even walked her to the school door.

Teacher Neal was standing in the aisle waiting to greet her. He said she looked like the flowers of the fields. "Starflower," he had called her. "That's you, Nadia. You are just like a "Starflower."

She had grinned all day.

Charlie was angry at first when she told him. But later, at supper, he said that it suited her and that was that. She had liked Charlie and Annie. She would miss them.

The first flakes of snow hit her face. She looked up at the sky again. The storm was closing in. According to her calculations, she should be nearing the pine grove. There would be plenty of wood to build a lean-to for the night. It would be small, but the lean-to would be fine for her. She was a small sturdy girl. As a young girl born in Alaska of strong parents, she knew the ways of her people well.

Charlie, too, was knowledgeable about the ways of the woodsmen. She was glad that he had shown her these ways. He was real proud of her learning ability. Most men would have laughed at her questions and walked away. Not Charlie!

He spent hours with her. Annie would be angry with them. Annie didn't like them to delay supper, but Charlie would always tell her to be quiet. "Nadia must learn," he would say. "She must know these things."

So Nadia had learned to build the lean-to and she had to learn to drive a sled. Charlie had made the sled for her. When she didn't think her first Christmas would mean anything to her, Charlie gave her Pookie and Pal. She found Lucky and Nanuk under the tree the next Christmas. Then, of course, there was her beautiful Nefra. She loved all her beautiful dogs.

The tears were coming faster down her cheeks. She swallowed hard. She must not panic now. Charlie, Annie, and the little store were gone, burned to the ground by two men who had come and pillaged everything they could find. They were big, dirty, and cruel!

She had been out running her dogs when she saw the smoke. When she came over the rise, she saw the store in flames. She froze. She could hardly believe what she was seeing. Charlie was lying on Annie in a pool of blood. The big man was standing over them. He was laughing a sickening laugh. The other man was putting Charlie's furs in the fancy car. When the backseat was filled, they drove away. She knew she had to tell Annie's brother, Lazlo, of the tragedy. He lived in Nome.

So Nadia turned her dogs and sled toward Nome. She was hoping the men had not seen her, but she had seen them. She would never forget the big man's face as long as she lived. She kept looking over her shoulder. She hadn't been seen. She made Nefra and the other dogs run faster until the scene was out of her sight.

The explosion shattered the silence of the afternoon.

"Oh, my God!" she screamed. "What was that?"

She looked up at the sky as she slowed Nefra and the

other dogs to a stop. Pookie was frightened in the trace and she petted him to calm him down. There was nothing she could do but watch as the plane spiraled down, toward the ground. She saw something come out of the rear door and land in the snow.

"The pilot! I've got to get the pilot!"

She started Nefra running. They came to him lying unconscious in the snow. She got him in the sled and took off racing toward the grove of pines. They were on her right about a mile ahead on the trail. Behind her, the plane exploded in a burst of flames.

Heaving a sigh of relief when she heard the injured man groan, she saw the grove of pines right before her. She slowed the dogs to a stop. The injured man groaned again.

She ran to the trees and gathered enough wood for the lean-to. After a few minutes, she had it made. She went back to the sled and lifted the injured man off and put him down gently on the furs she had smoothed out for him. She hoped she had not injured him more. After she checked his wounds, she covered him with the few other furs she had. She was glad when she heard him groan again. For now, his arm and legs would be all right.

Then she saw to her dogs. Pookie and Pal were worn out. They needed food and water first. Their paws were frozen. She took each paw in her hands to warm them. Lucky, Nanuk, and Nefra were next. Each one she petted, fed, and held them a moment, crooning an old Alaskan tune she had learned from her mother, to soothe them. Nefra twitched her ears and lay quiet.

The blizzard was coming in faster now. The wind whistled through the grove. The real storm was only moments away. She must cover the injured man again. He had tried to move and the furs fell away. She could see the blood staining his legs through the rent in his torn jumpsuit. There was nothing she could do except to try a simple bandage. His left arm was bleeding, too. She tore the hem of her blouse that she wore under her parka. She tried to remember Doctor Luma's instructions. She bandaged his legs and arm as best she could. Then she covered him with the furs again to keep him warm. She could feel his eyes on her all the time she was helping him. She gave a little smile to herself.

Then she reached for Nefra. As she hugged the big, furry dog, she saw the injured man close his eyes and go to sleep. She sighed a quick sigh.

"I won't be afraid," she thought as she felt Nefra's fur in her face. "Charlie told me never to be afraid. Afraid is to die!" Charlie was always right. "I'll be strong." She looked over at the sleeping man. Her big brown eyes gleamed. He groaned again. "Strong for you!" she whispered as she lay curled up with Nefra.

They were lying next to him so that she could hear him if anything was wrong during the night. She heard the blizzard swirl around the little lean-to. She worried a bit that the lean-to would blow away, but the little lean-to was sturdy and comfortable. She closed her eyes and put her head down in Nefra's fur.

Starflower slept.

The wind blew and rustled through the trees. Snow fell silently over all the earth. Once, during the night, the injured man awoke. He saw the little girl next to him. She was huddled on her fur parka and her dogs, asleep. He tried to smile. The pain came hard again and again. He looked down to see where the pain had started. He saw the simple bandages she had put around his broken arm. He tried to move his legs to ease the pain in them, but it was too hard. The legs just wouldn't move. He couldn't stand the pain anymore. He pulled the furs over his body and fell back to sleep.

The blizzard raged on.

CHAPTER 2

LONDON: NOVEMBER 1968

Grantwood Hall stood like a glorious gem in the center of snow-white diamonds. The land was level for miles everywhere you looked. The only lake was frozen over. The children of Grantwood Village, named for the great Captain Aron Grantwood who had sailed the seven seas in 1868 and had brought back treasures too numerous to count, were laughing, ice-skating, and throwing snowballs, fast and furious. Some more of the merriment was coming from the Great Hall that was lit up like Roman candles on a New Year's Eve.

There was a party going on. The Thanksgiving dinner dance was in full swing even though the evening was just beginning. Guests were slowly driving up the plowed road, carefully avoiding the snow banks along the edges, and gingerly backing up to the garage doors at the end of the cul-de-sac. Ladies wrapped their furs closer around their bare shoulders as the gentlemen hurried them up the great staircase to the lobby. Snow dripped from their boots onto a real Italian marble floor.

Amelia Grantwood Logan looked up from near the mantle where she had been standing, talking to some of her dearest friends. She was so glad she was wearing her burgundy velvet tonight. She was beautiful! The color was so right! The fit of her bodice was exactly the shape of her breasts. Men really noticed that! Not that it mattered to her anymore! She mentally shook her head. Joshua never looked at her now. Not since that afternoon! Oh, why had she gone to see that man? Gary! Such fun! She had been so happy! She smiled to herself.

They had such great times in his flat in London—all the lovely, exciting shows they had seen!—and the afternoons! Driving in the country! She had loved that most of all! Gary had kissed her! Such fire! She hadn't known she could feel that way about a man. She loved Joshua, but that feeling was so different! It made her weak in the knees, her skin tingle with anticipation. She closed her eyes so the tears wouldn't show.

She looked over at the couple coming in from the lobby. Gary! What should I do now?

The question went unanswered. She sighed and started toward the lobby. The dancers parted as she strode across the ballroom floor to greet the couple. She tried to smile. Gary took her hand. She shivered. He was so handsome! "Oh, Gary!" she sighed breathlessly, never seeing the girl on his arm.

The girl interrupted. Gary felt her squeeze his arm and turned to her. "Darling, get me a drink, won't you?" She hesitated, "Please?" Amelia looked away from Gary when she heard the girl's voice. She noticed how tall and blond the girl was. Almost as tall as Gary.

"Of course, my dear," Gary responded, laughing. "Coming right up. But first, let me introduce you to your hostess."

He turned to Amelia again. "This is Mary Lasher, my business partner's daughter."

Amelia nodded. He put his arm around the blonde girl. "This is Amelia Logan, Mary, your hostess. You know, Josh's wife.

Mary smiled and held out her hand to Amelia. "I think we've met before, haven't we?' Amelia smiled weakly. She gave her a hand. Mary shook it briefly. Amelia put her hand down and turned away. She remembered Mary had a crush on Joshua years ago. She didn't like Mary Lasher or her long, blond hair. Where was Joshua anyway?

She wondered when she didn't see him in among the dancers. She sighed again, following Gary and Mary into the ballroom. It wasn't long before she was dancing again. Every man in the room wanted a dance with the hostess of Grantwood Hall. She was flattered!

The gentleman in question was sound asleep in his upstairs bedroom. The din of laughter and music had not penetrated his room as yet. He was sleeping off the effects of the night before. Not that he drank so much in college, he didn't. He just couldn't hold it to one or two drinks. He always drank enough to make himself sick. It was his job at the bank, and being married to Amelia, that drove him to do it. He would never admit to himself that he was very unhappy or lonely. No! He couldn't do that. He was the director of a very large and solvent bank.

He had no time to indulge in emotions of the heart. He did try to show Amelia that he cared for her. Flowers, when she wasn't expecting them, candy she always gave to the children of the village, and little presents of some jewelry she had wanted, but no kisses. He wasn't that emotional!

Lately, he seemed to feel that Amelia ignored him. Whenever he would come into the room where she was holding court with her friends, she would be pleasant enough, but distant. Nothing he could put his finger on, just distant.

As for his bank, the takeover of Gary Lattimore and Roger Lasher's small bank was just a matter of expediency. The small bank was failing at a time when Grantwood-Logan bank was just starting to grow. In another year, it would rival the Bank of England. The Lattimore-Lasher bank had invested heavily in foreign markets, which had seemed good investments at the time, but had turned out to be big losers. Gary had begun to lose a lot of his properties. It was just a quick way for Gary and Robert to get out from under without losing everything they had. When Gary had come to him with the takeover proposal, Joshua knew he was at the end of his rope. So he decided to take the small bank and make it part of the Grantwood-Logan chain. He would make it a good investment in the long run.

Finally, the young man groaned and sat up. The crisp November wind was rattling the windows. He shivered. The fire was out in the fireplace. Where was Jameson? He wondered as he got up out of bed. He put on the navy blue robe he picked up from the floor. He never got tired of wearing this old velvet robe. His mother had given it to him one year when he complained of the cold in his room at college. (He missed his mother.)

He walked over to the fireplace, leaned over, and placed some pieces of wood on the grate. He took some matches from the trousers on the chair, struck one, and lit the wood. In a few minutes, the fire was going strong. He heard the music and clatter of dinner being served as the sound wafted up the staircase. He ran to take his shower.

Joshua was never ever late to dinner. It was a habit he learned early from his mother. He hurried into his clothes, making sure he was presentable: dark trousers, white shirt (no frills,) a red paisley tie, and dark jacket. He ran down the long staircase with the teak banister (brought from Burma by great-grand-father Aron) and entered the dining room. The food smelled delicious. Everyone was chatting happily. Jameson was serving the turkey and Elana, his wife, was pouring the coffee. The room exuded a cozy warm feeling. Joshua was in a better mood now, too. He even felt happy. He looked at his wife. She was so beautiful in the light from the great crystal chandelier blazing above the table. "Amelia, my sweet, I'm so sorry I'm late." He smiled graciously at her, then sat down in his chair at the head of the table. "I'll just sit here."

"Of course, Josh." She grinned, delighted at his appearance. He was so handsome, so tall, so strong, so like a little boy with his dark, curly hair falling down over one eye, just a little, so stubborn and unmoving, when angry. It was a trait all the Logan men had. To their wives it was very infuriating. But now, tonight, he was actually pleasant.

He was chatting with Roger and Lottie, her friends that she knew he didn't care for. He was even complimenting Jameson on the cook's turkey. The angry words they had earlier were forgotten. She smiled and ate, content with all.

She knew that tonight would be the last pleasant time they would have. Joshua had seen her and Gary on one of those memorable outings last summer. He had told her he was leaving in the morning. He had told her he had decided to fly around the world. He was going to take the Learjet up and give himself time to think. But now, he was happy, laughing at Lottie's banter and charming Elana as she served the coffee.

Amelia was ecstatic that her party was going to be a great success. It would be the talk of the cocktail set for many months to come.

Later that night, Amelia lay in the middle of her big four-poster bed with the pink and white quilt over her, feeling very much alone. Her heart lay in her chest like a great lead weight. The tears were streaming down her cheeks. Her breath came in short heaving gasps. Everything in her life was gone. Her mind was in a turmoil of emotions. He's leaving me! I can't do anything to stop him! Maybe I could talk to him. Would he listen to me? Her head ached miserably.

She threw back the quilt and ran across the room. She opened the door and ran down the hall to Joshua's door. All was quiet. She put her ear to the door to listen. Nothing. "Josh?" she called softly, tapping on the door. "May I come in?" no answer. Just silence.

"I just want to talk to you. Please?" She hesitated and listened. More silence. She tried the door. It was locked. She fought back her tears and ran back to her room. It was cold and drafty. The fireplace was out. She was freezing in the cold November wind that was whistling through the room. She rang for Jameson.

The knock came once on the door.

"Come in, Jameson." she said petulantly as he came into the room. He looked at her quizzically. He was never sure how to react to Miss Amelia and her needs. He stood at attention just inside the door. "Yes, Mum. What is your pleasure?" He waited quietly.

Amelia sat up in her big four-poster bed and tried to smile. "I need a fire, Jameson"

She spoke softly, trying to be nice. "And would you see where the draft is coming from? I'm so cold!" She huddled in the quilt and watched as he placed wood on the grate and lit it. The wood was dry. It sprang up into a glowing flame. The wind was blowing a drape at the far window that was open. He walked over and closed the open window quickly. After a few moments of checking the other window, he turned to her. "Is that all, Mum?"

"Yes, Jameson. Thank you. I really do think I'll sleep now." She turned and laid her head on the pillow. "Good night, Jameson," from the quilt. She looked at him from across the quilt. Softly, he heard her sigh. "Oh, Jameson, one other thing? Did my husband get to sleep? He wondered why she would ask a thing like that. He sighed. She always was a little peculiar. He frowned down at her, "Why, I really don't know, Mum. He was gone when I went to start his bath." He turned and went out saying, "Good night, Mum," as he closed the door.

Amelia was stunned. The loneliness filled her soul. Joshua had left right after dinner. He had never meant to say goodbye. The tears started again. She slumped down into her quilt and closed her tear-stained eyes. I'll never sleep again, she thought, but five minutes later, even the cold November wind banging at the windows couldn't wake her.

That blasted ringing! Somehow, she managed to come out of her sound sleep. She rolled over to pick up the telephone. "Hello," she grumbled. "Who is this?"

"Wake up, you sleepyhead," came the voice on the other end. "I want you to come over here. I miss you."

"Gary!" she laughed, fully awake now. "I'll be there. Give me an hour." The sound of his husky, vibrant voice sent shivers through her body.

She was there within the hour.

When he opened the door and stood there, clad only in a towel, she was numb with ecstasy. Her body quivered all over. She threw herself into his arms for a long embrace. She could feel his hardness against her thigh. He carried her into the bedroom, stripping off her pants and bra.

At first, Amelia hesitated. Then, as she felt his strong hands fondling her breasts, sending waves of shivers through her body, the thrill was too much. She gave in.

Her body was not hers, it was his. For the next few hours, they were lost in their passion.

Amelia moved with every thrust. A woman possessed. As she moved with Gary holding her, she knew she had to have this man. Joshua would have to divorce her. The thrusts came harder. They took her breath away. She lost herself in the pleasure. Gary thrust even harder. Then she felt him subside and go limp. She clung to him for a moment then let him release her from his arms. She breathed deeply. She was fulfilled now!

There was no tomorrow. Amelia was completely in love. She lay spent, sweat dripping down her legs, on the bed next to a sleeping Gary. He looked so handsome. She thought I'll never let him go. She sighed happily, and went to sleep, too. The tears and pain of Joshua leaving her were gone, forgotten in her passion of love-making with Gary Lattimore. She sighed again in her sleep.

Something slid down her cheek. It was sweat. She opened her eyes. She turned over and looked at Gary. He was still sleeping soundly. I must get out of here, she was thinking quickly, sliding out from under the cover. Her clothes were on the floor beside her. She grabbed them up in her arms and ran all the way across the bedroom floor, down the hall to the servants' bathroom.

The shower was refreshing, but quick. She was dressed and out of the bathroom in minutes. She ran downstairs and out a back door. The garden path was covered with light snow that fell during the early morning hours. She had to walk carefully around the corner to the little red sports car parked at the curb. The key was in her hand and she instantly opened the door. As she got in, her thoughts were in a jumble. What could she do now? How she wanted Gary! What about Joshua? That was the biggest problem now. She must talk to him when he came home.

She revved up the little red sports car and it sped down Old Wood Road to the crossroads where she stopped for the light. On the green light, she turned left up the Hill Road that was Grantwood Hall's main driveway. She sighed a little as she parked the little red sports car in its usual space. She got out and ran up the big stone steps. She looked around for people moving around. She saw no one as she took the circular staircase, two at a time, and reached her bedroom in five minutes. Jameson and Elana were still asleep.

That gave her time to sleep a bit more, too. She put her head in her hands and breathed a sigh of relief as she pulled off her slacks, panties, and shoes. They were wet from the rain that had started when she was in the shower earlier. She picked up the nightgown right where she had left it the night before. It only took a second to pull it on and then to climb into bed. Two seconds more and she was asleep.

For the next few hours, the Hall was quiet. As the day began, there came sounds from the kitchen. Elana was up and making breakfast for everyone while Jameson did the tray for Amelia.

Elana took the tray from Jameson. "Why don't you sit down to eat?" Jameson was pleased that she had put out his plate on the table. He sat down quickly and started to eat.

"I will take this up to Madam, then, I shall be down to eat with you, too," Elana said. "I'm sure she must be awake by now."

Amelia was awake and sitting up in her bed, prim and proper, as Elana came in with her breakfast tray. Along with the eggs, toast, and coffee, Jameson had put a small vase of flowers on it from the garden hothouse. He would always coax a small bouquet from the late bloomers for the Madam.

Elana looked quizzically at Amelia, wet dripping hair on her shoulders. And said, "Are you all right, Ma-am? You do look cold and you are shivering terribly." She put the tray down in Amelia's lap.

"I'm all right, Elana." She shook her hair. "I just washed it." She started to eat her eggs. "I'll bring the tray down later. Oh, when you go, please take those dirty clothes down with you. Thanks." She picked up her coffee and sipped it as she watched Elana pick up the said clothes.

Elana picked up the coat with the fur collar and, after a few shakes, hung it in the closet. She put the shoes in under the coat. She was surprised by the amount of dirt on them, but she said nothing. She'd seen Madam sneaking in and out many times. She did wonder who it was this time.

Amelia ate the eggs and toast. She was ravenous this morning. She felt her stomach rumble and she felt a bit nauseous. She shook the feeling off. She was deep in thought and did not notice Elana's strange look. She had no idea what problems she would have to deal with when Josh came home. All of a sudden, thunder and lightning flashed across the room. She grabbed the quilt and pulled it up to her chin. The tray fell to the floor, spilling its contents all over. Elana would pick it up

The cold November storm, along with trouble, was just beginning.

CHAPTER 3

THE FLIGHT: DECEMBER 1968

Joshua Bradfield Logan was very much at home in the air. The great Learjet took off with engines roaring. Heathrow Airport dwindled away as he rose to 30,000 ft. His thoughts were consuming him. He had been a Captain in the British Air Force for ten years. He had flown many types of planes.

Mostly fighters like the Super marine "Spitfire," but he did especially have a feel for the "F-86 Sabre" that had been flown in from North America. He had been fortunate enough to have taken it up at the end of World War II. A few of his flights were very severe, but he always made it back to the airfield. Some of his buddies even called him "Ace," but he was reluctant to carry the nickname back to Grantwood Hall. He didn't want to be reminded of the war or his part in it. Too many memories!

The Bradfields and the Logans were very prominent families in the Canadian province of British Columbia. When he was a small boy, he lived in the big Logan Plantation on Queen Charlotte Island. He would play for hours on the beach of the Pacific Ocean that was his front yard.

Francoise Logan was president of the small Vancouver Bank on Prince Edward Island and Joshua was often allowed to go with his father to the bank. Francoise Logan wanted his son to be a banker after himself. He would watch Joshua walking along beside him down the hall, enjoying Joshua's enthusiasm. He was glad that Joshua wanted to sit in the big chair, all the while, watching, listening, as the business of banking flowed around him.

Joshua was fascinated when he saw all the money the guards brought in. How eager he was to learn how to handle the accounts, too. He had a good grasp of the workings of banking. His father was proud of him. They had a good rapport with each other, father and son. As the years went by, he sensed his father getting restless. One day, when he was twelve, he walked into the big Logan Plantation lobby and saw his bags sitting on the floor. His mother's trunks and valises were there with his mother standing next to them, dressed for travel. Her eyes were sparkling with laughter. They were moving to London! The excitement was contagious. Joshua was caught up in it. He had always wanted to fly. He hurried to get ready for the trip. His father was coming to pick them up at any minute. It was a long way to the airport.

Lucille Bradfield Logan had the bluest eyes in all the province, her husband said. Now Joshua thought so, too. She reached down to hug him and those blue eyes smiled at him, penetrating his very soul. He loved his mother deeply. The closeness they had shared was with him still. He could still feel the joy in his heart as they flew across Canada. He had the seat next to her and she had answered every one of his questions. All the while her blue eyes sparkled with happiness. He knew she wanted this trip to be a success for them. His father seemed happy, too

The great Learjet engines hummed a tune all their own. He glanced down at his altimeter gauge and noted that he was climbing. He had reached an altitude of 40,000 feet. He leveled off and headed south. The lights of London and Heathrow Airport were falling away, disappearing in the distance. He knew he was over the North Atlantic Ocean. But all he saw was a myriad of stars winking past his wings. The engines droned on.

His thoughts carried him back to that fateful day in June. Amelia—and Gary Lattimore.

How could she be with him? He knew Gary Lattimore was a vicious and cruel man, in his business relationships and his personal ones, too. Amelia should have known how he felt about Gary Lattimore! He had told her often enough! But—how stubborn she could be! He remembered all too clearly.

They had met when his father had gone into partnership with her father, Amos Grantwood. Mr. Lasher had told Mr. Grantwood how well his father had done with his bank in Vancouver B.C. Mr. Grantwood offered his father a partnership in the great Grantwood Bank in London. That was the reason for the trip they took earlier. So now, Joshua had been allowed to go down to the bank that first morning when his father took over his office. He was very proud to walk along with his father, down the broad marbled floor of the hall, to the offices of the president and vice-president. That was his father's office.

As he went by the desks, counters, and teller cages, he saw the gleaming eyes and curly hair of a little girl coming around the counter. She ran right into him! He went down in a jumble of petticoats and arms, and dark, curly hair.

"Oh, dear!" she screamed. "Ha! Ha! Ha!" Laughing

hilariously, she shook out her skirts, and scrambled to her feet. He was slowly rising up, very angry. "Watch where you're going! " he yelled. They glared at each other.

"Aren't you going to apologize? What's your name? My name is Amelia. You know, Amelia Grantwood!" She let it all come out in a rush. Then she took a breath, stuck out her chin and struck a charming, little pose. The tellers, who had seen the two hit and go down, snickered, and went back to counting their money. They knew Amelia! Joshua was thunderstruck!

At twelve years of age, he was not all that taken with little girls. Particularly ones who had dark, curly hair and laughing, brown eyes and a bunch of petticoats. All the girls he knew wore jeans just like the boys. The Yukon Territory was a rough country to grow up in. No one put on "AIRS" back home.

From that day on Joshua was smitten. "I'm Joshua Logan." He answered calmly. He remembered his manners. "I'm glad to meet you, Miss Grantwood." Mother always told him to be nice to girls. "My father is going to work here. With your father, I guess." He was becoming more relaxed now.

"Oh, then I'll call you Josh." Amelia hesitated slightly. Then she put out her hand and took his. "I'll show you around, if you like?" She smiled sweetly and his heart gave a little lurch.

"Okay, " he said tentatively. "I'd like that."

And so, down the hall they went, Amelia chattering, pointing out rooms, even showing him the great vaults where they kept the money. Joshua just looked and listened. He was contented just to be near her.

One of the engines sputtered, breaking up his thoughts. The fuel gauge was showing a quarter full.

It was time to stay alert. He was over Cape Verde Island. The sky was beginning to lighten up to a dark smudgy gray. He would have to land at Sao Paulo to gas up and eat. Maybe, sleep a little.

Sao Paulo, Brazil! South America!

How many times he'd wanted to go there! Now he was on his way!

The Learjet was slowly dropping altitude. He must be careful landing this baby. The sky was still gray, full of clouds. He couldn't see the runway! The fuel gauge read almost empty and he had a moment of panic.

Then he saw the skyline of Sao Paulo and an airport runway just ahead. He pushed back on the throttle and the Learjet responded smoothly. He landed with no incidents. (He thought the right engine coughed a little.)

The airfield where he landed was a little way out from the center of the city. In fact, it looked more like a field of grass than a landing field. Everywhere he looked there was just green grass.

Even the skyline of the city in the distance was something to behold at early dawn. The soft tropical sun was just above the rooftops of the skyscrapers that loomed in the distance. He heard the muffled sounds of autos and the screaming of sirens as he walked across the green grass. This was a city of great industrial importance in Brazil. More than five million people lived here, worked here, loved here. Joshua was impressed. He had read about this city many times in his childhood. A small hanger loomed up before him. As he walked through the hanger to the snack bar, he smiled. The city was waking up. Not much different from London, only warmer!

At the snack bar he sat down on one of the stools, ordered breakfast from a cute little waitress, and sipped his coffee. He was tired. The flight, so far, had really been a drag. His mind was in chaos. The Learjet seemed smooth over Cape Verde Island, but sluggish a bit when he came in for the landing here.

After breakfast, he went back to where the Learjet was parked. He walked around it, checking it out. The cowling on the starboard engine showed a dark smudge—nothing otherwise. Nothing! Nothing that would cause such sluggishness. Engines are in good working order—running smooth—props ok. I wonder what could be causing it? He couldn't think anymore! He was too tired!

He went back to a small room in the back of the hanger. The mechanic's room, probably, he thought. He lay down on the bunk he found there. He needed a few minutes to rest. Five, maybe ten, and then he would be gone. It was seven hours to Tahiti. He wanted to land there in the daylight. He was asleep in three minutes and he slept the whole day.

"Hey, Man! You got to get out now." The mechanic was shaking him on the shoulder. "I got to close the hanger. Understand?" He kept shaking Joshua. "Come on, wake up! It's almost 7:00, Man. I got to go home now." The mechanic was sounding worried.

"Okay, Okay. I'm awake." Joshua grumbled. He sat up and swung his long legs over the side of the crude bunk. The nap had refreshed him a lot. He saw the mechanic hurrying across the hanger floor to the overhead doors at the far end. He was reaching up to pull them down when Joshua caught up to him. The doors came slamming down as the two men ran under them and onto the runway. Joshua grinned at the mechanic. He reached into his pocket and brought out some banknotes and gave them to the man. Then he ran to the snack bar.

The cute little waitress was still there. She smiled at him.

"How's for getting a ham sandwich and some coffee?" He saw a thermos on the counter and handed it to her with a dazzling smile. He had seen her start to close the door on him.

"Hokay, Meester. But you eat outside hokay?" She liked that dazzling smile. She hurried to make the sandwich and then filled the thermos with coffee. The coffee was still piping hot. "You go now, Meester. I close now." She said as she handed him the bag and thermos. He gave her a couple of pounds sterling down on the counter as she rang up his order and handed him the change. "You keep it." He yelled and waved to her.

Joshua ran across the runway to the Learjet parked at the fence. He never heard the "thanks, Meester," or saw her smile. He was ready to be on his way.

It was exhilarating to start the engines, swing around and taxi down the runway. He checked the weather conditions across Argentina and Chili. He was told that everything was normal. He leveled off again at 40,000 feet and headed into the darkened sky. Peru was ahead and then Tahiti. He would take a few days to rest there and think things through. He had to decide what to do about Amelia and their marriage. His mind was swirling. He couldn't think now. A few hours more and it would be morning. Winds were fair, the sun was hot, and no rain clouds in sight. Of course, that could change in a few hours, but for now, it was calm. It was a great day for flying. His heart was pounding. He pulled back on the throttle and the great Learjet rose majestically into the air. Ahead lay clear blue skies. Five hours of watching the lush tropical jungle of Argentina pass by under him, and having eaten the sandwich and drunk some of the coffee, he reached over and put the Learjet on autopilot and went to sleep again.

The engines coughed, sputtered slightly, and Joshua woke up with a jerk. He had lost some altitude. He checked the instruments and looked out over the land. He was watching for the coast of Chili and the blue of the Pacific Ocean. He had been thinking about the sluggish starboard engine, but every sound he heard now, was smooth and regular. If the turbine was not getting enough fuel or oxygen to it, he couldn't hear it. Well, he would check them again when he landed in Tahiti.

When he saw the coastline of the ocean up ahead, he thought of his home on Queen Charlotte Island. He wondered if the old plantation was still intact. Had mother moved back there after his father had died? He hoped that she had. He would visit her again, one of these days, he promised himself, after he completed the takeover of the Lattimore-Lasher bank. He knew the Lashers, Robert and his daughter, Mary. She was always hanging on him, wanting him to do her homework and walk her home, when all he wanted to do was to be with Amelia. Finally, he had to tell her. He was going to marry Amelia. Mary threw a fit at first. She got drunk at one of the parties the four of them would attend and then she met Gary Lattimore, the son of his father's bitterest enemy.

Joshua would never forget the day his father had come to him and told him Lattimore, Sr. was foreclosing on their plantation. His father told him that he had borrowed the money from the Lattimore-Lasher bank to move them to London. He put the Logan Plantation up for collateral. The loan went through without any problems. His father then found out that Lattimore, Sr. had bought out the Vancouver Bank. Lattimore, Sr. had called in the loan for late payments. It never occurred to Joshua that his father was having trouble paying back the loan.

Joshua was only seventeen. All he knew was that his mother cried a lot and his father was all worn-out and old looking. He knew his father liked to play cards, but then, everyone in his father's crowd played. Sometimes the stakes were very high. The men who came to the Logan Plantation liked to boast about how much they had won. His father never smiled at that. He would just pick up his drink and leave the room.

Joshua did notice his father drinking too much. He had come home early from school one day and found his father drunk in the kitchen. That's when his father blurted out the news of the coming foreclosure. Mr. Lattimore was demanding his money. His father didn't have the four month's payments. He had lost it to the men he had played cards with several nights ago. His father passed out. Joshua took him up to his room and put him to bed. Then Joshua went back down to the kitchen. He sat down to think what he could do to save the plantation. His mother loved it so much. It had always been their home. Finally, he had made a decision.

He wondered where his mother was!

The next morning he found her in the kitchen making him breakfast. "I heard you moving around." She said quietly. "Did you know your father told me about our losing the plantation?" Joshua looked at her and shook his head. "Yes, Mother, he did tell me everything." He didn't know what else to tell her. What he had decided he couldn't tell her at that moment. He would wait until later. "I have to go to the bank this morning, Mother. I'll have some news for you about the foreclosure when I get back. Father is sleeping upstairs. I will talk to you both at dinner tonight." He ate his eggs and coffee and ran out the door.

He went to Mr. Lattimore at the bank and told him what he had decided. He would pay his father's loan. He would work for Mr. Lattimore in the bank. Mr. Lattimore resisted the thought of Joshua working for him. But Joshua kept telling him how he could make the bank grow and prosper. His father had prepared him well.

In the end Mr. Lattimore took him in and sent him to Vancouver, B.C. to work in the little bank where his father had started out. He worked fourteen hours a day and Mr. Lattimore took half his pay. Joshua worked hard and never complained. After a few years he made the bank solvent. The customers loved him. They remembered when his father had worked there.

Joshua told his parents what he had decided that night at dinner. His father was devastated by this news. He knew it would be many years for Joshua to pay all the money back. Joshua had gotten the plantation back, but at a terrible cost. The years it took him to pay off the loan were too much for his father. The drinking got worse. His mother stayed in her room most of the time. But she would come out to eat with him. His father never came out of his room. He just gave up.

Summers in London were warm, windy, happy days for Joshua. He would come home from the bank with all kinds of lovely plans for his mother. They would drive up the coast and lunch in Northhampton. Sometimes his mother would say she wanted to sit on the beach, she missed the beach in front of the plantation, so they would drive to Brighton Beach for a day. They would always ask his father to go with them, but he would always say no.

The Learjet was coughing again in the starboard engine. He glanced down at the gauges again. All the gauges were showing normal. There was nothing to suggest any trouble. He wondered what it was that made the engine cough. He shook his head. Only the blue water of the Pacific Ocean was below him. The island of Tahiti must be coming into view soon. He would be glad to see it.

He went back to his thoughts. The last day in the summer of 1959 Mr. Grantwood and Amelia came to see his mother. Mr. Grantwood took his mother into the library. He went over to Amelia who was standing at the window looking out. She was so quiet, so lost in thought.

"Hello. Amelia." He said, smiling. "I'm delighted to see you!"

Amelia turned to him and gave him a small grin. "It's nice to see you, too, Joshua." He took her hand and led her to the sofa along the wall. Right away they were in deep conversation. Amelia loved to swim and they were deciding which beach to go to. They finally decided to go to Brighton beach. They sat quietly holding hands and waiting for his mother and Mr. Grantwood to come out.

His mother and Mr. Grantwood were in the library a long time. When they did come through the door, Joshua saw that his mother was crying. Joshua hurried to her. "Mother!" he exclaimed anxiously. "What is the matter?" He put his arms around her as she tried to hide her tears. "You must be brave and try to understand." She paused a moment, then went on. "Your father was under much stress."

She started to weep again. "My dearest, your father shot himself early this morning. Mr. Grantwood found him. Oh, Joshua, your father is dead!" She was gasping for breath. "I'm so sorry!" He still had his arms around her. He held her close as he tried to hide the shock.

He held in his grief. He couldn't break down now. He just couldn't. "Don't worry, Mother. I'll go with Mr. Grantwood and help him take care of things." He wasn't sure what to say next. He could feel the tears welling up in his eyes, too. He brushed them away as he looked at his mother in his arms. "Poor Dad! I'm sorry, too." His voice broke. "Oh, Mom! Please don't cry! He loved us! You know he did! You must remember that, he loved us!" Joshua wasn't sure his mother was listening so he just held her a few moments longer. Then Amelia came over and took her upstairs.

Joshua called the doctor who said he would come right over. The doctor was as good as his word. He came a half hour later. He checked Mrs. Logan for shock and gave her a sedative after he heard the explanation from Joshua. "The sedative will take effect immediately. Your mother should sleep for several hours." The doctor told them. Amelia said she would stay with her. Joshua was grateful for that. The drive to Brighton Beach would have to wait.

Mr. Grantwood got up from his chair and walked out to the hall where he picked up his hat and cane. Joshua went with him. He knew he had to go down to the bank and clean out his father's desk. It was not a pleasant task for him. There were too many memories. He was silent the whole time as the Grantwood limousine sped on. Mr. Grantwood tried to tell him of his father's last day.

He told Joshua that he was surprised to see his father come in. It was supposed to be his day off.

He saw his father go to his office and never saw him alive again. When he heard the shot he went to the office and found his father dead. He had called the paramedics immediately. They came within a few minutes. They checked his father's body then took him to the morgue. The medical examiner would do an autopsy there and let Joshua know the outcome the next day. Joshua knew what the outcome would be. Death was caused by a shot in the head. Mr. Grantwood finished his narrative and looked over at Joshua sitting beside him. Joshua never said a word.

Joshua finally said, "There is not much else to do. I will just have to make the funeral arrangements later. Mother is completely devastated now." He shut his tear-stained eyes and put his head back on the seat. He stayed that way until they arrived at the bank.

Mr. Grantwood and Joshua walked into the lobby filled with customers doing their usual daily transactions. Joshua went past the teller cages and down the hall to his father's office. As he opened the door, a flood of memories came to his mind. He saw the big chair he used to sit in as he watched his father working on bank business. He knew everything that was on the desk—some important papers, the photographs of mother and himself, a trophy that his father had gotten when, as a boy, he had won a fishing contest back home in Canada. Joshua put them all in a box he found in the corner of the room and carried it out to the Grantwood limousine. Then he went back in and made the call to the mortuary manager who told him he would take care of the arrangements for the funeral. That was Friday, the funeral would be on Sunday. His heart was broken. But he would not give in to his grief. He knew who had caused his father's death. Somehow, someday, he, Joshua Logan, would atone for it. The Lattimores would be through when he put his plan into motion. He blinked back the tears.

The engines on the starboard side started to cough. Joshua checked his gauges. He was losing some oil pressure and dropping altitude. He took the Learjet off autopilot and looked around. He was over the coast of Chili, heading for Tahiti. He could see the trees in the distance. He was sure the engine had lost some fuel. He decided he had better land soon. Tahiti was straight ahead—the gleaming sand beach stretching along the shore. The heat haze was low to the ground. He was glad to see the runway cleared for him to land. He looked down and realized the runway was too short for the Learjet.

He pulled back quickly on the wheel and gained altitude. He was seeing the Society Islands below. He couldn't land there.

It was a two-day flight to Tahiti. He hoped the starboard engine would stay running. For the time being, everything sounded normal. The turbine was humming smooth so the oxygen and fuel were getting to the combustion chamber. He stayed alert all night and the next day. About the middle of the afternoon of the third day he saw the shoreline of Tahiti Island, shining like a great jewel, emerald and diamond against sapphire. He saw the runway ahead and landed the Learjet smoothly. He came to a stop right in front of the tower. He bent over and put his head on his arms. He had made it, so far.

Tahiti!

The beach was deserted this time of day. It seemed that all the inhabitants went indoors when the heat of the afternoon got up to the 100s. Joshua was lying on this particular stretch of sand, quietly contemplating the flight of a seagull out over the ocean. The ocean was a brilliant blue, like his mother's eyes. The waves were lapping at his feet, then running back out to the water. Never slowing, always the same, whitecaps coming, then going. It was peaceful here.

Joshua decided to stay until dark. Although the sun was burning his skin, he was not going to get up. Okay, so he was being stubborn! Also, sunburned! Finally, he got up and went back to his room. The first thing he did was to call the airport and get the mechanic on the line.

"How's my plane?" he asked the man who answered. "I'm Josh Logan"

"Can't find anything wrong, sir." The man said. "If it was in the compressors, we would have found something." The man paused, then went on. "We checked everything we could."

Joshua thanked him and heaved a sigh. Three days here and the Learjet checked out all right. Funny! He had really thought something was wrong. "Okay, have it gassed up. I want to leave in the morning." He put down the telephone.

The dining room was all lush tropical plants and flowers. Joshua almost forgot that back home in London it was beginning to snow. It was early December. Almost Christmas! Like all children of all ages, he liked the Christmas season.

He had married Amelia on Christmas—once. Amelia! What was he going to do about her? When he got back home, they would have to talk. He looked down at his plate. He wasn't hungry. He wanted a drink! He had a taste for brandy, in fact, several brandies!

The brandies were taking his depression away. He felt light as a feather. He decided to call London and find out about the takeover he was planning. His manager at the bank told him the takeover was going along smoothly. Gary Lattimore and Robert Lasher were committed to the deal. They were not making any trouble. It would be completed by Christmas. Joshua gave the manager some last minute instructions, hung up the telephone, and finally sprawled over the bed and went to sleep. Tomorrow he would head out over the Arctic and the North. He would be home in London in time for Christmas.

Joshua was drunk! He knew it even before the sunbeam hit him square on his face. He opened his eyes, then, quickly closed them. He rolled over on his side. His head throbbed like a million hammers were pounding his brain. The waves of nausea swept over him. He groaned.

The bathroom was across the floor. He made it! More nausea! His stomach flip-flopped. Finally. The eruption! He never felt so bad! His stomach flip-flopped again. More nausea! More eruption! "This is too much!' He cried, thinking of his father. "Oh, Dad, why? Why did you do it?

The tears came streaming down his cheeks. Again he was the little boy back on Queen Charlotte Island. His heart cried. His grief seemed endless. His stomach flip-flopped again.

The nausea was not so severe this time. Nothing came up. The pain in his head eased. He made it to the shower. The hot steaming water revived him. "Oh, Dad, we could have worked it out."

Joshua was feeling much better now. He dressed and went

down to breakfast determined to find out why Amelia had become so distant to him. On the stairs, Amelia's face floated before him. He gave in to his thoughts. She is so beautiful and I do love her. We can work it out. He had to know what had changed her.

The thought remained as he sat down. After some toast, orange juice, and coffee, he felt like he could fly again. After the second cup of coffee, he was ready to go. The phrase, We can work it out! ran through his head. We can work it out! He smiled a little smile as he left the restaurant.

The early morning sun was hot on his back. It felt good. In fact, since he had come to a decision about his life, and about Amelia, everything was good. He looked down where the Learjet was parked on the runway. He was glad to see it. He smiled as he walked toward it. All the while, he was thinking, I will be home for Christmas!

CHAPTER 4
THE FLIGHT ENDS: ARCTIC, ALASKA 1968

He gave the people around him a smile as he walked to the tower. The Learjet was right where he parked it. He walked over to check out the starboard engine. It seemed to be a bit dirty in the turbine and around the cowling. Otherwise, it looked okay. He gave the wing a little pat as he climbed in.

He taxied down the runway, asking for the weather conditions for flying north. He was going across Alaska's northern tip, the North Pole, and he wanted to be sure of good weather all the way.

The voice on the radio told him—fair conditions until he got over the Bering Sea. There was a storm front coming through carrying a lot of snow, four, maybe five, hours away. He could wait it out or go more easterly over the Alaskan chain. The weather over the Gulf of Alaska was better, only rain predicted there. Prince William Sound and the Panhandle predicted the same. Rain!

Joshua knew he should wait it out. But he was eager to be on his way. He pulled back on the throttle and the Learjet rose smoothly into the air. He passed the tower and flew right into the sun. The bright blue of the Pacific Ocean spread out below. The lush green vegetation and clear blue lagoons of Tahiti were soon left behind.

He put the Learjet on autopilot and laid back to rest. He ate the light lunch he brought from the restaurant. The hot coffee helped him to relax. He was getting sleepy. He dozed in the warm cockpit as the plane soared through the sky.

He felt a little air turbulence as he passed over the Hawaiian Islands, crossing the Tropic of Cancer as he headed north. It must be the sign of that storm from the Bering Sea he thought. It was becoming colder now. He went to the storage area and found his heavy Air force jumpsuit and helmet. He quickly put them on. Good old Jameson! He remembered!

Several hours later, he saw the Aleutians dead ahead. He took off the autopilot. The clouds indicated the storm was coming in. They were black, smudgy clumps in the sky and they were pulling in a fierce wind. It was getting cold. Very cold! He was glad he had on his jumpsuit and helmet. The wind whipped the wings up and down like a branch on a tree. He struggled to keep the Learjet level.

All he saw on the horizon was snow. Snow! Fluffy white snow! All around him in the cockpit! Even on the ground.

Suddenly, the starboard engine quit. Something exploded!

Joshua grabbed for a parachute but he was too late. The Learjet was going down, spiraling towards all that snow. He had to get out now! 20,000 feet! 10,000 feet! Down and down!

As the plane got closer to the ground, he managed to get to the rear cargo door. He figured he could make it if he fell out into the snow, using the snow like a mattress. He waited until he was a few hundred feet from the ground and jumped. The nose of the Learjet hit the ground at the same time he did and burst into flames. The snow cushioned him as he landed.

He felt the excruciating pain in his arm and legs. He lay there for a long while, letting the snow hit his face. The pain was almost too much for him. He passed out for a few minutes and then he was awake again. He felt warm hands on his face wiping away the snow. He felt the slight movement as he was being carefully lifted—the pain was so overpowering! He blacked out!

CHAPTER 5
ON THE WAY TO NOME: DECEMBER 1968

There comes a time in everyone's life when there is a turning point. It is not a sudden thought or a burst of energy. You just go to sleep one night, satisfied with all you did that day, and wake up the next morning knowing you are changed. Something is different with you. Everything has a new meaning for you. As sure as night becomes day, Nadia "Starflower" Charles knew that she had made the turning point in her young life.

She knew the minute she woke up and looked into two very glistening brown eyes looking back at her. Her whole body tingled under her fur parka. Her face lit up in a happy smile. Her injured pilot was awake. For the first time in two days he was aware of her. She saw the pain, but he was lucid.

He sat up slightly. "Where am I?" his voice was deep, strong. He wavered, winced as his strength was going. The pain deepened. "Who are you?" His voice was not so strong now. He slumped down again. He tried to sit up again. He couldn't. He tried to talk again. He couldn't do that either. The weakness and pain overcame him. He just lay there, looking at her.

Starflower put her hand on his shoulder and made him lie still. The crude bandages she had made for him would not stay in place if he moved too much .She was very glad she had learned to take care of the animals that always got caught in the hunter's traps. She would always bandage them when they were brought to the little store at Fort Yukon.

That was how she came to have her lovely Nefra.

Starflower had found her caught in a vicious bear trap one day. She had struggled for hours to free her. She had only been nine years old and not very strong, but she had released the pup from the trap and carried her all the way home. Nefra was only ten months old. She had been running in the field that year and had become lost from her mother.

Charlie had showed her how to bandage her leg and somehow Nefra had healed. They were inseparable from then on. Right now, Nefra was twitching her ears, waiting for Starflower to pet her. She smiled, putting her hand down on Nefra's head.

She was hesitant to talk, but she decided to tell him what he wanted to know. She spoke softly. "I'm Starflower. You are on a tundra in Alaska. If you are up to it, I'm going to take you to Nome." She paused. The brown eyes kept looking at her. She took a deep breath and went on. "I have to talk to the men there. My uncle is there, too," She stopped talking and looked over at him.

He had closed his eyes now. He was very weak. Maybe she should wait a little longer. She looked out at the sky. NO! They have to be on their way. The sky was darkening again. More snow!

She asked him quietly, "What is your name?"

His voice came from the furs, "Josh Logan. I came from London, in England." His voice died out.

Starflower knew he was not able to talk more. She must get him on the sled. She must get him to Nome as soon as possible. What she had not told him was how badly he was injured. She didn't know how to tell him his legs were gone and an arm was broken. The arm would be all right with care, but he would probably never walk again. His spine was smashed. She would let the doctor in Nome tell him that. For now, she would treat him as normally as she could.

"Josh Logan, from England." She breathed, almost whispering. "You are a long way from home, Captain." She smiled suddenly. She had seen the insignia on his jumpsuit. Charlie had told her about them, too. And about the planes that had flown over the little store.

His head came out from under the furs. He grinned at her. Then, as the effort of moving his arm caught him, he realized how weak he was. He lay back again under the furs. She made sure he was as comfortable in the sled as she could make. She admonished him to lie still and go back to sleep, if he could. She covered him with the rest of the furs she had used for herself during the night. She went to get her dogs. She watered them, fed them what little food was left, then hooked them up. Pal and Lucky close to the sled, then Nanuk and Pookie in the middle so that Pookie wouldn't lag. Then Nefra. Her lead dog was anxiously pawing the snow. She was waiting for the order to move out. Starflower yelled the command and they were on their way.

The snow was deep and covered the lean-to, but she had dug it out the day before and there had been no new snowfall overnight. She glanced back at the grove of pines and felt a twinge of sadness. Her little lean-to had been a good home for two days. She looked down at the pile of furs on the sled. Her passenger was asleep again and she was glad of that.

Starflower knew her trail across the tundra was not going to be easy. She needed all her strength and energy to control the heavy sled and the dogs that were racing along at breakneck speed. She slowed them down to a reasonable pace with a command and covered five miles that afternoon.

There were hills that were splendid exercises for the dogs, but she worried every time the sled made a sudden jerk. It took all her strength to keep the sled level and running along. Every now and then, she would hear a groan from the furs and knew her passenger was awake.

It was early evening when she pulled into the small village of Galena. The people of this small village were delighted to see her pull in. They did not get very many visitors to their village because they were far from the towns that were to the south of them. They ran up to the sled and saw the pile of furs. When her passenger poked his head up, the villagers laughed and started to get him out of the sled. She had to step in and stop them. They would have hurt him if they had continued to lift him the wrong way. She didn't want them to break the bandages she had made. She would tell them her story later.

The Community Hall was opened and the villagers carried Joshua very carefully into the larger room and put him down by the big stone fireplace. With the furs that Starflower had wrapped him in he was quite warm and comfortable. After Starflower and Joshua had eaten the simple, delicious meal prepared for them by the villagers, Starflower told her tale.

It was hard to talk about Charlie and Annie, but she did the best she could. Then she told them about finding Joshua. And it really frightened the villagers when she told them about the plane exploding. Joshua was getting tired and slumped down into the furs. In a moment he was asleep. Joshua slept most of the time she was talking, but he woke up to hear part of the story. It did not mean anything to him at that moment, so he put it out of his mind. He was more amazed at how friendly these Alaskan people were. He wanted to hear all about them, but there was no time now. They wanted to know all about him, too. He promised to come back to visit them again someday. Then he would tell them all about the big city across the world from them. They all laughed and shook his hand and patted him gently on his shoulder when he told them he really was a Canadian from Queen Charlotte Island!

Starflower was amazed and delighted to hear this news, too. She would ask about it later. She had learned about Queen Charlotte Island from the hunters that came to Charlie's little store for their supplies. She was always asking them questions about the rest of the country she knew was out beyond the door of the little store.

Joshua groaned. Starflower could see his strength was going. He just lay there groaning as the villagers talked. He had talked too much. The pain was taking its toll. He must rest or he could not go on. She finally got him settled down for the night with the help of the Elders of the village. He slept quietly.

The snowstorm that had started early was blowing, so Starflower had decided to wait out the night. She knew her pilot needed the rest. Starflower was tired, too. She told the villagers how grateful she was to have their help. They could see that she was nodding off. They told her that they would feed her dogs. She must not worry about them. Just to get some sleep, too. She would have a long, hard journey tomorrow. They would give her enough provisions to finish her journey to Nome. She was thankful for their kind and thoughtful gestures.

She lay down beside Joshua, listening to him breathe steadily. She finally fell asleep, but just before her eyes closed, she thought she saw two brown eyes looking at her.

It was not yet light when she heard the screams. Her pilot was dreaming. He thrashed around under the furs. She knew he would disrupt the poor bandages that held his arm and legs together. He was taking a turn for the worse. Suddenly he was quiet. She saw that he was not moving. He was unconscious.

She scrambled out of her bed of furs. She ran out into the snow to the house of the old lady the people had called "The Healer." She knocked and knocked. The kindly old face showed through the crack in the door. The cold was fifty degrees below this night and the old lady didn't want to leave her warm house. She was irritated at being disturbed. Starflower begged her to come and look at her injured pilot. "Please?" she was crying.

The old lady threw up her hands. "All right, all right. I come."

She put on her parka and leggings, then, pulled on her Mukluks. She went out the door and waddled down the road to the Community Hall where Starflower and Joshua were bedded down. Starflower ran behind. The Old Healer took one look at Joshua and told Starflower he had gone into shock. She pointed out to Starflower the clammy skin, his pale blue lips, and shallow breathing.

"Just keep him warm and don't move him," she said, piling more fur blankets on him.

"He is badly injured, is he not?" looking at Starflower's anxious face.

Starflower nodded, "Yes, Old Healer, he is." She went on, explaining what she could. "His arm is broken, I think. I have tried to bandage it. His legs do not move—but I was careful putting him on the sled. I have not moved him much at all. He does not know about his legs." She hesitated a moment, then went on. "I cannot tell him what I think. I only saw him fall out of the airplane. Old Healer, I am worried about him. I do not know much about helping him." Starflower finally stopped talking. She looked at the Old Healer intently.

The Old Healer had listened just as intently. When Starflower took a breath, the Old Healer started to talk. She had made a decision. All the rest of the night and into the early dawn she told Starflower of her old healing methods, handed down from generation to generation in her family, all the while administering to Joshua. Slowly his breathing became smooth and regular. Starflower relaxed. She put her head down on the fur blankets next to Joshua and went to sleep. The Old Healer just sat there, watching Joshua.

The next morning as Starflower lay asleep in her fur blankets, the Old Healer was still sitting nearby, watching them. She was secretly glad that she had told this young girl her healing methods. Now there would be someone to carry on her traditions. She knew her time was short. After listening to Starflower explain the injuries last night, she knew Starflower would carry on her work. She had told Starflower to go to college when she was older.

There was much more she needed to learn about healing. The Old Healer had told her she could learn it all if she put her mind to it. She saw the same ability in Starflower that Charlie and Dr. Luma had seen. She sat watching her two new friends sleeping. She thought and prayed as she rocked in the rocking chair the villagers had brought for her during the long night. The wind whistled across the tundra.

As the morning sun came up and the wind quieted down, Starflower awoke. She rose and shook the Old Healer, who looked up, grinned, and stood up to stretch. She gave a quick look at Joshua, gave a few instructions to Starflower about his food. Then she waddled off down the road to her little house that was almost buried in the snow.

Starflower and Joshua were alone. Joshua slept on. He was breathing regularly now. Starflower gathered up some wood to make a fire in the big stone fireplace that was at the back of the Community Hall. It was not long before the room was warm. She went back to Joshua's side and sat down. She sat with him all day. She did not eat very much from the good food the villagers had brought her. Always, she kept him warm, soothing him with her singing when he became restless in his pain. Joshua could feel her warm hands on his face.

Toward early evening he was awake. He looked around. He saw her at the big stone fireplace. Her back was to him. "What was her name?" He could not remember at first. He kept thinking. Finally, out it came. It didn't sound like his voice. "Starflower." He whispered, then a little louder. "Starflower." He thought he had yelled. Actually, he had said it normally.

She heard his deep quiet voice and turned to look at him. Her heart was racing in her little body. He was awake!

Now he could see her clearly. Small sturdy body, dressed in a fur parka, a lovely face with big gleaming brown eyes, and when she raised her hand to push back her hood, shining dark hair. She was smiling at him, a dazzling smile. He never noticed how young she was.

"Yes, Captain Logan?" she asked anxiously. "What is it? Are you a little better now?" She went to him.

"Oh yes, Starflower. I am much better now." He paused then went on. "Do you know? I believe I'm hungry!" He smiled at her and tried to sit up. He slumped back on the fur blanket and quickly said, "Could I have some of that soup now?" He tried to sit up again but couldn't.

The pain was too much for him. His legs and his arm were really throbbing. Starflower saw the pain in his eyes. She knelt down to help him sit up. She propped him up against the wall. Then she filled a bowl with soup and handed it to him. He couldn't hold the spoon. He tried to eat with his good hand, but he was too clumsy. Before he could spill it all, she took the spoon and fed him. He ate it all, laughing and wincing between every bite. She couldn't help but laugh with him, too.

After she cleaned the dishes, she told him to rest some more. She needed to see to her dogs. She had not been able to look after them. Joshua needed her attention more. When she went out, she found that they were fed and content. The village children had taken over their care while she was busy inside. The children were playing with them, petting them, and getting ready to run them around the tundra. Starflower ran with them for a time, glad to be free of responsibility for a while. She threw some snowballs at the children and they threw more back. All the while, they all just laughed.

The sky was beginning to darken. The children said they had to go in. It was their suppertime. Some mothers were already calling. They ran off, still laughing. Starflower was left with Nefra and the other dogs panting in their traces. She hugged Nefra, putting her face down in her fur. She thought of all the Old Healer had told her.

She decided she would go to college if she could afford it. Of course, she would have to wait until she was eighteen. That was only two years away. She never told anyone her birthday was today. Charlie and Annie always celebrated it on Christmas. She had liked that. She shook her head. She had to put those memories out of her mind. It hurt too much to remember.

She started planning her next leg of their journey to Nome.

Joshua seemed much better now and the snowstorms had died down. It would be a good time to start out tomorrow at first light. She loaded the sled with her provisions and furs the villagers had given her for Joshua. She had no reason to stay now. It was a two-day ride over rough hilly tundra with scattered creeks all along the trail. These creeks must be frozen solid or they would be impossible to cross.

That night, at supper, she told Joshua her plan. He was in agreement with her. He knew he must get to Nome for medical help that Starflower couldn't give him. He had found out the night before, that when he tried to move his legs, all he felt was intense pain. He could not move them. He couldn't walk! He was grateful to Starflower for treating him as a normal human being, but he knew he wasn't. He was as anxious as she to be on their way.

And so, the next morning, the sled and dogs, with Joshua bedded down in the furs and Starflower running behind guiding them, moved out across the tundra that was covered by new-fallen snow while the villagers all waved their goodbyes. They had wished the two travelers well. They knew the dangers of the journey Starflower was taking. It was a long, arduous journey to Nome, especially in early December.

On the first day out from Galena, she followed the Yukon River down to Unalakleet. Joshua was tired from the rough journey. It was hard, very hard, for him to come to the realization that he couldn't move his legs even though he would try as he lay under the furs watching the dogs run on over the hard-packed snow. Starflower watched him. She felt some of his frustration, but she said nothing to him.

"Mush, Nefra, mush," was all she would say. Nefra ran on smoothly. Pookie, Pal, Lucky and Nanuk followed smoothly behind Nefra's lead. Starflower followed in their paw prints. It was difficult to keep the sled upright, but she was managing it fairly well. Joshua stayed as quiet as he could to help her. He was amazed at her strength.

At Unalakleet, she told the people there about Charlie and Annie. She also told them about the terrible men who came to the little store at Fort Yukon. Because these men of Unalakleet fished for whales and sold the products they made in Fairbanks, she warned them to be careful of men who drove a big, fancy car. They assured her that they would be very watchful of the men. Then they showed her where they could sleep. Joshua listened to every word Starflower was saying. He tried to keep alert, but he was too tired and in very much pain. She knew he had to be bedded down for the night. She was so tired! She was gazing at the sky when she heard Joshua sigh in his sleep. She was grateful for the night. She slept soundly.

The next day she told Joshua they were going to follow the low-lying ground along the shore of Norton Sound. All the little creeks were frozen. She pointed out White Mountain as they passed by. The sled swooshed smoothly along. Joshua was very impressed by the beauty and grandeur of the Alaskan terrain. He had never seen such mountains and beautiful sunsets before. And snow! Never so much snow! Oh, how he wanted to get out and play in it. Just like when he was a kid in Vancouver. Someday he would do it! Someday!

He turned and smiled up at Starflower. He never knew a girl like her. He was sure he would never forget her. She looked down at him and smiled back.

For some time now, these two needed no words between them. There was a bond that had grown between them that would never be broken.

Starflower headed up the trail toward the little village of Council that was not far from Nome. The snow flurries were becoming like a blizzard. They obscured her vision.

Once she almost lost the sled and Joshua in a snow bank, but finally, the flurries blew away. She was able to see the little village in the distance. Joshua was groaning very heavily now. She knew she had to get him there. She tried to reassure him that he was going to be taken care of. He was going to go home to England.

She saw the seaplane at the dock and knew the Bush Pilot was having coffee in the little cabin on the shore. He was sitting in the window and waved to her. She hailed him as they pulled in. Nefra slowed her pace to stop in front of the door.

The pilot came out yelling questions so fast at her that she could only wait until she had made Joshua try to get up enough to be helped out of the sled. He tried, but couldn't. The pilot saw him try and ran over to grab him up. He carried Joshua into the cabin and put him down on the bed in the corner of the room. Then he turned to see Starflower walk in. He asked her for information on what had happened. She explained as best she could.

The pilot's wife made Joshua a sandwich and gave them all cups of coffee and as he ate he listened to Starflower tell the pilot that his injuries were very serious. He had to be flown to Anchorage Hospital as soon as possible. Joshua needed to be flown to London, England where he could be in his own hospital where he would get the care he needed. Could the Bush pilot help her?

The Bush pilot assured her he would do everything to make Joshua comfortable. He would radio the hospital in Anchorage to be ready for them when they landed. He knew the message would take a few minutes. He told Starflower to eat and rest. She refused. She had to go.

She said, "Goodbye, Captain Logan. I know you will get better after you get back home." She smiled that dazzling smile at him as she went out the door.

Giving a sigh of relief, and only looking back once as she left the little village, she knew she had done all she could for Joshua. He was being held up by the pilot and his wife. She saw him in the window. She saw him give her a small wave. The little gesture gave her heart a twinge. She smiled to herself. Then she was past the cabin. He was out of sight. She was on her way to Nome to find Uncle Lazlo, Annie's brother.

The snow lay white ahead of her all the way.

THE UNBROKEN BOND

PART TWO

TWENTY YEARS LATER

CHAPTER 6

RECOGNITION: NOVEMBER 1983

In her office at London General Hospital, Dr. Nadia Charles stood looking out at the rain-spattered street. She was watching the evening traffic heading away from downtown. It was cold. Ice was forming on the cars parked in the parking lot below. It would be hazardous driving tonight. She mentally prepared herself for a busy time in the "ER."

Now she was enjoying a moment of peace and quiet in her "Inner Sanctum" as she was prone to call her spacious office on the third floor. She was thinking about her job. She was very proud of her appointment as Hospital Administrator. Her teacher and friend, Mr. Neal, had helped her to get into college. He gave her every bit of encouragement along the way. He even managed to see that she interned in Anchorage at Humana Hospital. And he made sure that she was considered for the position at London General. It took several years for her to graduate.

Mr. Neal was so proud of her. And she graduated with honors.

The English doctors were very skeptical about accepting her, but finally one day, she received the letter of acceptance. It was a very pleasant day in May five years ago. She had been overjoyed! Mr. Neal had helped her pack for the trip to London. She had never been out of Alaska in her whole life. She was a little overwhelmed! But Mr. Neal made sure she was on the right plane for New York. The airport was so large she didn't know where to go to get on the plane. So many people! So many suitcases! So much noise! But in the end, she had been delighted that he decided to fly there with her. He told her he had family in New York that he hadn't seen for awhile

She also had to take a ship to England so he had made all the arrangements for her cabin. It was a beautiful sailing. She would never forget the ocean and skimming over the waves. At night, it was absolutely glorious! But she was remembering that she cried a little as she watched the ship back away from the dock and she realized that she was alone. She was going on the biggest adventure of her young life. For a while she looked back at New York in the distance. She thought of Mr. Neal. He had been so very dear to her!

She sighed, then turned and walked around her big walnut desk and sat down in her big leather chair. The files lay on the desk before her. She picked one up and opened it. Smiling a little, she saw that it was Joey Reardon's file. His mother had brought him in, screaming his head off, holding up his arm. It was broken. He had fallen off his bicycle. She had quieted his screams and soothed his mother's fears all the while putting on the Plaster of Paris cast. When she had finished, Joey went chattering down the hall hanging on the hand of his mother telling her he would have every kid in his homeroom sign it. She closed the file and dropped it into the basket on the corner of her desk.

She picked up the next file and opened it. Oh yes. The very frightened young man!

He had been diagnosed with the AIDS virus. She sent him to Dr. Stives for his treatment. Dr. Stives immediately put him in the ward on the second floor. She hoped he would be sleeping now. She would look in on him later. She closed his file and put it in the basket with the Joey Reardon file. Nurse Jacobs would file them in the morning. The last file was the one she didn't want to see. But, knowing her duty, she picked it up and opened it. As she read the name, the memories came flooding back. Joshua and his wife at the "Society Bazaar," Mrs. Logan speeding down the avenue in her little red sports car.

Then, that awful day!

Joshua was dedicating the Grantwood-Logan wing for the handicapped. It was for people like himself, the paraplegics, who needed specialized treatment. The hospital needed this equipment badly, so Joshua had given the best. Nadia was very happy for this wing.

When the ceremony was over, she had gone to the cafeteria for a quick coffee break. As she was coming from the line, she ran right into him. His wheelchair was so quiet that she didn't hear it coming into the room. She held tight to her cup of coffee so as not to spill it on him. He glanced up at her with no attempt to speak to her. She looked at him and realized that he didn't recognize her. She just went on by toward her office.

There was a commotion in the hallway. Mrs. Logan had come in with a group of her friends. Nadia watched as everyone crowded around Joshua. The congratulations seemed to please him. He was gracious to everyone. He looked up at his wife standing next to him. She was smiling and leaned down to kiss him lightly on his cheek. There were several men shaking his hand. Nadia knew one of the men was the Prime Minister. Nadia suddenly realized how important a man he had become. He thanked everyone and looked up from the handshaking. His wife put her hand on his shoulder. It was time for them to go. He turned the wheelchair around to face the doorway. He saw her standing in the doorway.

She saw him look at her. A slight, quizzical look passed his eyes. She almost went over to talk to him, then, hesitated. The crowd grew larger and louder. She heard her name over the intercom. The moment was gone.

The file was heavy in her hand.

She had just finished signing the death certificate. Amelia Logan—that beautiful, vibrant woman had just been killed in an auto accident. The report had said that she was driving too fast in the rain. She had lost control of her sports car. The car was totaled. She was DOA when the paramedics brought her in. The police had made out their report after she had made a very detailed examination of her body. Now they were gone.

Nadia closed the file and laid it down on her desk. She looked across the room and saw Amelia's mink coat lying over the couch arm, glistening in the evening light. Her diamonds were locked in the wall safe, waiting for Joshua to come and take them home. He would be here soon she thought. She sat down to wait for him.

She had called one of the numbers she had been given by the police. The butler told her that Mr. Logan was out. The butler would give Mr. Logan the message as soon as he arrived home. She thanked him and hung up. She sat back in her big chair.

The evening traffic was gone now. Her office was quiet. There had been many times over the years that she had contemplated this meeting. Her hands shook a little as she waited. She clasped them tightly.

The footsteps rang loudly in the hallway.

"That's not Josh." She thought. She quickly pushed back from her desk and rose from her big chair where she had been sitting. She went back to the window. There was only one car in the parking lot now. It looked familiar, but it was too dark to make out any distinguishing features. Besides, that was a long time ago—1968—as if she would ever forget that year!

Even as she turned from the window to look at the face of the man who entered, she knew. She knew every little feature of that face and that ugly, sickening laugh. She knew this man who had killed Charlie and Annie. She knew. She waited. Would he know her?

"Dr. Charles?" his deep voice penetrated her very being. "I'm a friend of Amelia Logan. The nurse at the front desk told me to see you." He held out his hand, elegantly gloved. "I'm Gary Lattimore. I would like to see her, if it's possible." That sickening smile again!

He did not know her!

"How do you do, Mr. Lattimore." She answered, very cool, not shaking his hand. "You will have to wait. I must speak with her husband before I can issue any order of visitation. As you can see, he has not arrived yet." She turned her back on him. "You may wait in the lounge. If you wish." She dismissed him curtly She walked over to the window and waited for the sound of the door to close. When she heard him leave, she let out a sigh of deep relief.

So, that was his name—Gary Lattimore! After all these years!

CHAPTER 7

A HOMECOMING: THEN AND NOW

The bush pilot held Joshua up for the few moments that Starflower ran down the trail toward Nome and out of sight. He could feel Joshua slipping from his arms. The pain was getting to be more severe now. Joshua was moaning loudly. He had to get Joshua back to Anchorage as soon as possible. His wife didn't know how to fix the soaked bandages. He had to hurry!

They managed to lift Joshua into the small plane and the bush pilot told his wife that he would be back in a few days. Then he revved up the engine of the small plane and pulled away from the dock. He flew Joshua from Council to Anchorage without any problems. There was some turbulence over the interior and a snowstorm was developing out over the Bering Sea but they were too far inland to be affected by it. The bush pilot took his bearings calmly as he looked down at Joshua lying on the floor beside him. Everything was as good as he could make it for Joshua, so he followed the coastline down to Anchorage. It only took a few hours.

In Anchorage, Joshua had the bush pilot call the Humana Hospital. They would make all the arrangements for the flight over the ocean to London. The nurse could take care of the simple bandages that Starflower had put on so many days ago. He kept seeing those big, gleaming eyes looking at him in his sleep. He shook his head to clear it. That was a long time ago. He had to get back home now. When all the arrangements were made and he was settled in the airplane, the nurse from Humana Hospital tucked him in on the gurney and sat down by his side. The next feeling Joshua had was the lifting off of the big airplane that was taking him home.

The lights of Heathrow Airport were visible to him as the pilot banked left and started his landing approach. Joshua felt a sense of exhilaration when he heard the bump of the landing gears drop into place. He heard the screech of tires when they hit the runway as they were coming to a stop.

Home! He could hardly wait!

The nurse eased him onto a new gurney with the help of the paramedics who had been called and were waiting for him. He looked up to see where Amelia was. He couldn't see her anywhere. The paramedics were pushing him back and urging him to lie quiet. Where was she? He was tired, but he wanted to be the first to see Amelia when she came into his view. The nurse had told him she was coming!

Finally! He saw her walking toward him. She saw him at the same time. She started to walk faster toward the gurney. She saw how much he had changed. She wanted to cry. Pride wouldn't let her in front of the nurse and the paramedics. She leaned over him. He could smell her perfume as she gave him a small, light kiss. In the ambulance she held his hand all the way home. He could feel the pressure of it just before he passed out.

Joshua spent the next five years in and out of the hospital. There were times when he would be at the bank, but the bank practically ran itself under the supervision of his staff. Mostly he kept in touch by telephone. He was never able to see Amelia for very long so he never had the opportunity to talk to her about his decision for their life together. But after this last bout of pneumonia, he felt certain that he had to say something to her soon.

Joshua looked out his window and waited for Amelia to come. He was going home today! Again! The pneumonia was gone and he was feeling good. The sun was shining. The trees and grasses of the parking lot were as green as they could be. It was spring in London! A little breeze fluttered the curtain at the slightly opened window. He loved spring in London. He felt like leaping out of bed and jumping for joy. He had missed Grantwood Hall and Amelia. He would tell her so when she came. He tried to move his legs. Nothing! He wanted to scream! He lay quiet, sighing. He tried to resign himself to the thought that he quite likely would never walk again.

Dr. Charles said he needed lots of therapy and London General didn't have the proper facilities for all the help he would need. He had told Dr. Charles that he would build a new wing for all the equipment he would buy. He was going to be the first to use it. She had been doubtful at first. Then she was delighted. He smiled to himself.

He had been quite amazed when she introduced herself as the Administrator of London General. She had seemed so young. But, since the Board of Directors had chosen her, he would abide by their decision. Even though he was a director too, he was just too weak to disagree with them. She did such a good job for him, too. She was always there when he needed help with his therapy.

He thought back to that day in the cafeteria. Something had struck a cord in him.

He couldn't remember. Dr. Charles had seemed different to him. But she went out the door and he forgot the feeling.

A sound in the hall made him turn his head from the window and look to the door. Amelia walked in. Her beautiful dark hair flowed about her head as she came striding over to the bed. She always knew how to make an entrance. He raised his arms to hold her and waited for the usual welcome kiss.

"Come on, Josh. It's time we were going." She smiled at him suddenly. "Elana will have the dinner ready before we get there if you don't hurry." A sound at the door made her turn. Nurse Jacobs was bringing in his wheelchair. "I'll do that, Nurse Jacobs." Amelia said graciously as she took the wheelchair from the nurse and pushed it up to the side of Josh's bed.

Joshua was stunned! Amelia never did anything for him since he came home from the last time he was in the hospital. He got into the wheelchair as best he could. His legs seemed like sticks as he tried to swing them around. After a brief struggle, Nurse Jacobs helped him to settle in comfortably. He hated it, but managed a slight smile for her. He turned to Amelia with another little smile. "Okay, Let's go. I don't want to keep Elana waiting." He started out the door. Amelia followed.

Later, when he and Amelia were riding in the limousine with Jameson driving, he told her about his decision. His head was throbbing.

"I have decided to be a more loving husband to you, darling." He squeezed her hand as he looked at her tenderly. "The cool afternoon air was soothing his headache. "I have given up my drinking, too. I—" He hesitated a moment. "I am hoping you and I will have a much happier life now." He waited for her to answer. Her hand was very warm in his. She never moved it.

She said nothing. She couldn't.

All the time he was away, she had waited and planned. She wanted a divorce. She wanted to marry Gary Lattimore. Oh, how she adored that man! His lovemaking took her breath away. She gave him passion for passion every time they were together.

And that was every afternoon! Now their secret meeting would have to wait. Joshua was home! She heard Josh's voice, but she didn't hear the one word she wanted to hear. Slowly she turned from the window. She looked at him with a small smile. How she loathed Joshua!

"That's wonderful, dear Josh." She lied. "I'm so glad to have you back." She gave him a whisper of a kiss on his cheek and turned again to look out the window. She couldn't let him see how devastated she was.

The limousine sped down the tree-lined avenue. The artists were busy painting the scenes of the river Thames. Joshua watched as the strollers mingled around midst all the clutter. The warm breeze eased his throbbing head. He felt like a kid again. Even the pain in his legs seemed to disappear as he listened to the happy cries of the children playing along the bank.

The limousine sped on.

Soon the sun glinted on a large building up ahead. Grantwood Hall! Home! He really was home again. Sun was shining through the trees and lighting up the windows with a glow he thought he would never see again. The sunset hurt his eyes. It was so beautiful!

It was a marvelous display of golden rays. Then, as suddenly as it was there, it was gone.

Night had fallen. The moonlight brought out the severe lines of the battlements of Grantwood Hall like a pen and pencil drawing. The limousine pulled up to the steps of the portico. Elana was waiting with the rest of the staff. They were all glad to see The Master so well. He waved to them. Jameson waved them back inside. Elana stayed, waiting quietly.

Jameson came around and opened the door for Joshua. He was going to help Joshua out, but Joshua shook his head. He would do it himself. Amelia got out and ran around the car to him. He waved her back out of the way. He eased his legs out onto the ground grasping the sides of the doorjamb. As he lifted himself up to stand, the pain in his legs gave a sudden quick twinge. He started falling. Jameson caught him. Amelia hurried to help. She put her arms under his and held him against the limousine as Jameson got the wheelchair opened. Joshua sat down in it gratefully. Elana saw the incident and started to cry. She turned and went up the long steps. Jameson carried Joshua up the long steps, too. Amelia followed quietly carrying the folded wheelchair with her. At the top of the steps, she opened the wheelchair again and Jameson put Joshua in it as softly as he could. They made their way into the lobby. Joshua said he wanted to go to his room that was at the end of the long corridor.

At dinner, Elana still had tears in her eyes, but quickly wiped them away as she served the sumptuous meal she had prepared for Joshua's homecoming. Amelia made a special effort to show her pleasure at having Joshua back. Joshua ate very little. He was very quiet. He was discouraged to realize that he could not even stand by himself. He promised himself that someday he would learn to stand again. For now, he would master the wheelchair better.

When they were finally in their room, Amelia made him comfortable in the big bed. She gave him a small kiss and lay down beside him. In a few moments, she was asleep. Joshua looked down at his sleeping wife and decided she was still the most beautiful woman he had ever seen. He pulled her into his arms and held her close. He could feel the warmth of her body next to him. He wanted to make love to her. But suddenly she became restless in his grasp and turned away. He let her go. She gave out a little sigh as she curled up into a deeper sleep. Perhaps he would try again later.

His thoughts then turned to the business of his bank. He had been neglecting that phase of his life lately. He should be checking on the final takeover program of the Lattimore-Lasher bank merger. He needed to get back on track now that he was well again.

He was so happy he could hardly relax. But as he lay there listening to the night breezes rustle through the trees in the garden, he became drowsy. His last thought before he dropped off was that Dr. Charles and Nurse Jacobs had done their jobs well. He would try to walk again! And then he, too, was sound asleep.

Several months later Joshua sat at his desk in the bank, Big Ben was booming out the evening hour. He looked down at the record books he held in his hands. He had been balancing the accounts and counting the money that the bank kept in the vault. Ever since he had taken over the Lattimore-Lasher Bank accounts, he had noticed a shortage of cash in the vault after Gary had been put in charge of the accounting department. Several times he had checked the books, but always, the money had checked out. But not tonight!

The books showed a balance of forty-two million dollars, but the actual cash in the vault was only showing forty-one million dollars. That meant one million dollars was missing. The money was gone! He had checked and double-checked. The money was really gone!

He sat there, wondering what he should do. Should he confront Gary? Should he call the Securities Commission? Should he call the police? Right now, he didn't want to do any of these things. He would wait. Let Gary convict himself. But how?

The money had to be put back into the vault by Monday morning. That gave him the weekend to make Gary admit to taking it. Joshua was so sure of this fact that he let his mind run over the last few weeks. He remembered Mary Lattimore spending much more money than he had surmised that they really had. Mary's spending was even noticed by Amelia. Just the other day she commented on her extravagance.

The telephone rang. He picked it up. Jameson was on the other end. "Sir, you have a message from London General Hospital. You are requested to be there to see a Dr. Charles. It's about your wife, I believe." Jameson was breathless. Strange! He was always the perfect butler, so cool, so unflappable.

"All right, Jameson." Joshua answered. "Calm down and pick me up as soon as you can."

He hung up. Now what has Amelia done? He thought to himself, I wonder how bad it is.

Outside the snow was starting to fall. Joshua rolled himself to the service elevator and pushed the button to go down the three floors to ground level. Jameson was there waiting. He rolled to the door of the limousine and Jameson opened it. He lifted himself up to get in and found that he couldn't do it. After another try, he had Jameson lift him in, angry at being so clumsy. Jameson put his blanket over his legs and took the wheelchair around to the trunk. He put the wheelchair in the trunk and closed it. Then he walked back to the driver's side and got in. The limousine started up with a purr. They hurried to the hospital.

Nadia was watching the snowflakes cover the parking lot with a blanket of white. She was remembering another land with a blanket of white. Nome! And her dogs! Dear old Nefra! Uncle Lazlo! He had been so kind to them. He had taken her and her dogs in and loved them as if they were his own.

For the two and a half years she had stayed with him, she had been happy. It had been the nicest home she had ever known other than Charlie's little store. Uncle Lazlo had made her almost forget all the pain and loneliness of the tragedy in Fort Yukon.

But she did miss her injured pilot!

The men of Nome had gone to Fairbanks to help in the rebuilding of that city. Uncle Lazlo had gone to Fort Yukon to bury Charlie and Annie. He sold the land the little store had been on. He got a good price for it. He put the money away for her schooling. Between Uncle Lazlo and Teacher Neal, she had become what she was tonight. The Head of London General Hospital!

How she loved London General! Every time she did an operation on a child or held the hand of an elderly man or woman in the middle of the night she felt a kindred spirit with these English people. Since she left Nome and Anchorage she had been very much alone. At London General she was at home. This hospital and these people were her family now. She turned from the window as Nurse Jacobs put her head through the door.

"Hi, Nadia." She said, grinning. "I've just closed down the front desk for the night. All the calls were transferred to "ER." Care to have a cup of coffee with me before we get started in the Zoo?" Nancy always, laughingly, called "ER" the Zoo. Probably because of all the people who showed up there every night.

"No, Nancy." Nadia smiled. "Thank you. I would love to, but I have to wait for Mr. Logan to come in." She looked at her watch. "He should be here anytime now." She gave out a small sigh. "I'm not looking forward to giving him the bad news." She gave Nancy a quick wave.

Nancy backed out the door "Okay, I'll see you later!" She gave Nadia a slight wave back as she hurried down the corridor.

The elevator door slammed open. Nadia heard the swish of the wheelchair as it came gliding down the corridor. She came around the corner of her desk to stand in front of it. She just stood there waiting. Fifteen years had not changed her that much. She was, of course, taller, a little thinner, but still the same Starflower.

When Jameson pushed him through the door, Joshua saw her standing there. She waited a little longer. The recognition was not there.

The woman Joshua saw standing before him now was the woman he knew as Dr. Charles, his midnight friend, who held his hand when he couldn't sleep, who always had a smile or a cup of coffee when he was tired and restless after the awful therapy. So many times he had felt her hands on his face as he thrashed in bed trying to get up. And always, she had soothed him. Now he sat there silent, waiting to hear what she had to tell him.

Nadia started to talk. "I'm very, very sorry." She took a deep breath. Her voice sounded hollow in the room. "Mr. Logan, I really dread having to tell you this." She took a quick breath again. "Your wife was killed in an auto accident earlier this evening." She hesitated. She was waiting for him to say something.

Joshua was shocked. The words wouldn't come.

Nadia went on. "Your wife was speeding on Brighton Beach Road. She lost control of her sports car." She paused, turned, and walked around to her big leather chair. She sat down. She was quietly looking at Joshua's expression. Joshua's face went white. Nadia could see he was having difficulty getting his thoughts together.

Jameson leaned over him. "Are you all right, sir?"

Joshua looked up at Nadia, then at Jameson. He nodded slowly. He took a deep breath. His voice came out deep and confident. (The voice she would always remember.)

"I'm all right now, Jameson." He had tears in his eyes. He wiped them away with a brush of his hand. "My wife always drove too fast." He smiled wanly at Nadia, looking around the room. "I see you have Amelia's mink coat. I'll just take it, if you don't mind."

Nadia went over to the couch and picked up the mink coat. The fur was soft against her hands. She walked over to Joshua and laid it in his lap. He ran his hands across the fur. His eyes were suddenly far away.

He blinked and looked up at Jameson. "Jameson, please go down and bring up that old valise from the trunk."

"Yes, sir." Jameson said as he left the room.

Nadia went to the safe and brought out the diamonds that were twinkling in the plastic bag. She handed the plastic bag to Joshua. He just put them in his pocket. He kept stroking the fur and looking at her now. Nadia saw the quizzical look come back into his eyes. He kept looking at her with those glistening brown eyes she had grown to love. She still waited. It had been a long time. He had been through a lot. Perhaps—someday—he would remember.

The clang of the elevator door broke the moment.

Jameson came in followed by Gary Lattimore. "I just heard." He put a hand on Joshua's shoulder. "Poor Amelia. I only came in because the police called me when they couldn't find you at home." He paused then went on. "They found my number in her purse." He grinned that awful sickening smile Nadia knew so well.

Gary was noncommittal about it. He had nothing to lose. He had already told Amelia that he had married Mary Lasher. As far as he was concerned Amelia could get lost. He had told Amelia that he and Mary were having an affair before he had met Amelia. Amelia had known the night of her Thanksgiving party many years ago.

Now Mary had come into a lot of money and he was

going to be on Easy Street. He was leaving Grantwood-Logan Bank. He had hated the job. He had turned over the accounting department to Mary's father, Robert Lasher.

Joshua clenched his fists as he stayed there and listened. He knew that Gary was incriminating himself about the money. He was incriminating his wife, too. He was getting very angry. In fact, he was so angry he was shaking. There was never a time when Joshua believed that Amelia was unfaithful to him. But now, Gary Lattimore had brought it out into the open. Joshua was not going to have Gary destroy Amelia's name tonight.

"How dare you insinuate my wife was unfaithful? Joshua was shouting, trying to get up out of the wheelchair. "Get out of here. Leave me alone!" He kept struggling to stand up.

Gary laughed that ugly sickening laugh and shrugged. "Okay, Josh. I'll see you tomorrow." He went out. They could hear him laughing all the way to the elevator.

"Calm down, Mr. Logan." Nadia sounded like Dr. Charles now. She was worried that Josh would have a heart attack. "Please control yourself." She knew only too well how fragile his health was now.

Joshua was ashamed of his outburst in front of Dr. Charles. He was a very influential man in London, a prominent banker, and here he was, shouting like a child. The loss of Amelia had, all of a sudden, hit him.

Gary's words had brought it all back. The afternoons she would come in for lunch and then the three of them would go to the beach or out into the countryside. Gary was always there in the background. She had implied it was just a pleasant coincidence. She had insisted (the last time they had talked about Gary) that she was not seeing him anymore. Obviously, she had lied.

He had begun to wonder lately why she would feign

illness whenever he wanted to make love to her. And the times when she did let him, she was very unresponsive. He had tried to make her happy, and for a while, he thought he had.

He felt the fur against his hand. So soft! She loved the mink coat. He had given it to her last Christmas. She always said it went well with her diamonds. Now, it doesn't matter. Maybe he should give it to his mother. "No." he thought. "I'll give it to Elana. She will care for it. She deserves it." He stroked it once more. Then he looked up at Jameson. "For Elana." Jameson was speechless for a moment. "Thank you, sir." He said in the most respectful manner he knew. "Is there anything else, sir?" He took the mink coat from Joshua's lap. He carefully folded it and put it in the valise.

Joshua shook his head. "No, Jameson. We'll be going home now."

He turned to Nadia. "Dr. Charles, I will make the funeral arrangements for Amelia tomorrow. Will two o'clock be all right to pick her up?"

"Of course, Mr. Logan." Nadia was very professional. "We will have her ready then. Good night, Mr. Logan."

Joshua and Jameson were already to the door. Her last words ran through his mind. They were very haunting words. Had he heard them before?

Jameson wheeled him around and out to the elevator. Again she heard the swish of his wheelchair as they went down the corridor. Nadia sighed deeply, saddened by Joshua's apparent weakness. She had remembered a strong, virile man.

She looked at her watch. Time to go to work.

She was holding Amelia's file in her hands. She gave it one quick look and closed it. She dropped it in the box with the others and went out. She hurried down to "ER."

She had been right. The driving had been hazardous. The people milled about. "ER" was full.

Nancy Jacobs raised her head as she came up to the gurney where Nancy was helping a small girl in pain.

"Welcome to the Zoo!"

It was a clear cold day in the cemetery.

The limousines lined the curb on both sides of the drive in front of the Mausoleum. Joshua's black limousine was parked right at the walk so that he could wheel himself up to the door without any trouble. He was sitting there by the limousine waiting for Jameson to push him into the sanctuary for the service. He looked around at the people who were standing there waiting to go in. Most of them he didn't even know. Of course, there was Roger and Lottie, her dearest friends. And his mother was just to the left of him. Her face was stoic. She looked down at him and tried to smile. She put her hand on his arm. He knew she was not happy with Amelia. But she always treated Amelia with respect when they would visit her

He couldn't see Gary and Mary Lattimore in the crowd. For that, he was glad.

The sanctuary was warm. The flower arrangements were gorgeous. Mother really knew how to decorate he thought.

The minister droned on—"Ashes to ashes, dust to dust...."

Joshua's mind remembered back to that Thanksgiving party so long ago. Amelia had been happy then. He wanted to remember her that way. Not that silent, angry woman who rode home with him in the limousine. Oh, she was mad that day—he knew why now. He knew when Gary had taunted him in the hospital. Poor Amelia! How lost she must have felt driving down that Brighton Beach Road! Rejected by someone she really had loved! Joshua shook his head quickly, bringing himself back.

The minister was saying, "Amen."

Then he felt his mother press his shoulder. "It is time to go, Josh. I will get Jameson to help you get to the grave." She did smile then. "It was a lovely moving service, wasn't it? You looked so far away. Did you like the service?"

"Yes, Mother. I thought the service was beautiful. Pastor Moss was very good with his presentation. I was just remembering." He quickly turned to look for Jameson.

Jameson came hurrying up to them and started pushing Joshua out to the sidewalk and down to the grave. When they got there, Joshua saw the other people standing around silently praying as Pastor Moss said the last rites. Amelia was laid slowly down into the ground.

Roger walked over to him and shook his hand. "I'm sorry, Joshua." He went back to Lottie's side and took her hand. She was crying, wiping her eyes with her tissue. She never said a word to him.

Pastor Moss stopped talking. The last rites were done.

The people walked by giving him their condolences. He thanked them all.

Then Jameson pushed him back to his limousine. His mother got in and then Jameson helped him get in. He was grateful for it. His mother turned to him. She patted his hand. There was no need for words. He felt her love, just as he had felt it as a boy going to London on the plane, in that small gesture.

As they drove away, Joshua couldn't help thinking how beautiful Amelia had been. How vibrant! How tormented! He had never suspected how tormented she really had been! He should have guessed. But he was always too busy to notice. Until that one day when he caught them!

He closed his eyes, trying to forget. Now she was at

peace. He would only remember her that way. He laid back his head.

All the way back to town another face kept coming into his mind---a lovely little face with dark gleaming eyes and shining hair.

The snow fell silently as they drove. He was remembering a ride in falling snow. Sluicing along, wind in his face, snow covering his fur blankets, a soft voice crooning to her dogs. "Where was she tonight?" he wondered. Suddenly, he knew, as never before, he missed that little face and that soft voice.

Would he ever see her again? Would he ever see Starflower again?

His mind rejoiced!

He had remembered her name!

CHAPTER 8

A CUNNING PLAN: OCTOBER 1986

It was Autumn on Queen Charlotte Island. The trees were turning red and yellow. The clouds were beginning to darken. There would be rain soon. The breeze was freshening. He noticed the leaves turning from dark to light as the wind fluttered them.

Joshua stood on the porch of the old Plantation house and marveled at the changes of nature. He marveled at other changes, too. He thought of the one he made for himself. He had worked hard to make this change. The therapy was finally paying off. He would walk again! He was beginning to tire. He knew he would have to rest, but not just yet. He heard a sound behind him. His mother came out and stood with him.

"Your father always liked this time of year," she said softly.

"I know, Mother," he answered as he sat himself down gingerly into the wheelchair. He looked up at her and saw those beautiful blue eyes looking up at the sky. "Are you all right, Mother?" he asked concerned.

She smiled at him and nodded. "I'm just fine, son. You are here. Elana and Jameson are here. I am home at last. It's just wonderful for me. I've really missed being here. Now, I have my things, my treasures, around me and I am happy."

The wind fluttered the trees. The clap of thunder sounded in the distance. The sky darkened some more. She looked at him, wondering if she should ask.

"Are you happy, son?" she asked wistfully. "Really happy?" she didn't wait for him to answer, just went on, "You know, I am so proud of you. I do think you will walk a little, soon. You have come a long way in these last years." She patted him on the shoulder, then turned and went back into the house.

What a question to ask him? Of course, he was happy. But he knew down deep in his soul that the happiness was just an illusion. His life was empty. Most of the time, nowadays, was spent in the bank or at the hospital in therapy. He had finally learned to stand again. It had been a lot of hard work. There was no time for anything or anyone else. He liked it that way. He told himself Amelia was gone and he had finally gotten used to being alone. Even liked living in the apartment in town. It was close to the bank and the hospital. He had closed Grantwood Hall. He just couldn't stand living there with all the memories.

At the townhouse he only had Jameson to take care of him. He had his books. He loved his music. Every night he would read a little and listen to his music. Often, he would remember another tune, another little voice crooning. Another time.

Then he would think of Mary Lasher. She would always be hanging on every word he said when they were in school.

Until Amelia! Why had she married that Gary Lattimore? He sat back down in the wheelchair, thinking.

One summer, around the time of the missing money, they (Joshua, Mary and Gary) had gone on a cruise with Mary's father, Robert. They had gone to Bermuda. According to Mary's father, she had paid for everything, Not Gary! Joshua was stunned by this news. The Lashers had lost everything they had owned in the takeover of their bank years ago. He had Robert working for him now. So where would Mary get money for cruises? And how could she afford a man like Gary Lattimore? Everyone knew how he spent his money. Gambling, drinking, and Joshua knew of several large investments that went broke. Gary had lost a bundle!

Suddenly, Joshua sat bolt upright!

A picture came to his mind. He was sitting at his desk going over some accounts. Robert had the vault open. He was getting some account books for him. Mary was sitting at her father's desk when Robert called to her. He wanted the records that were on his desk. He was going to put them in the vault when he came out with Joshua's books. She had gotten up and taken the records into the vault to her father. Robert brought out the account books he had asked for and put them on his desk. Joshua never paid any attention. He just picked up the account books and started to read them.

A few minutes later, Mary came out of the vault with a briefcase. He had assumed it was Robert's. Her father was often carrying papers home with him. Nothing was unusual about that. Joshua had forgotten the incident until now.

Before he could call the police he had to have proof. He would have to ask someone to help him. He knew he could count on Jameson. But who else could he trust? He thought for a moment, Dr. Charles, of course.

When he got back to London he would talk to her. She

would have to know the whole situation that Jameson knew. Jameson had found some money wrappers in the service elevator that night when he came to take him to the hospital. That awful night!

The wind began to gust and it was getting chilly on the porch. He rolled himself into the big cozy living room and turned on the TV. He was enjoying one of his favorite shows when Jameson came in.

"Your dinner is ready. Mrs. Logan sent me to bring you in." Jameson took the handles of the wheelchair and pushed him down the hall to the dining room. Elana had made his favorite roast and potatoes. He could smell the delightful aroma all the way. Jameson wheeled him to his place at the table. His mother filled his plate with food and put it down in front of him.

"Have you thought about what you are going to do with Grantwood Hall?" His mother was curious. "It is still a beautiful place. All of Amelia's treasures are intact." His mother took a bite of food and looked at him. She did know that he had closed Grantwood Hall after Amelia's funeral.

Joshua looked at the food on his plate. "Yes, Mother, as a matter of fact, I have made a decision about that. I know when I closed it that it would remain empty for a time. I am really sorry about that. All those treasures that Captain Aron brought home from his voyages should be seen by everyone, so—I have turned Grantwood Hall over to the village to be used as a museum." He grinned at his mother as he put a piece of roast in his mouth. "What do you think of that?"

His mother glowed with delight. "That's a splendid idea, son. I rather like it!" she said as she took a sip of coffee. "It's such a beautiful place. So many gorgeous treasures! It will be a perfect museum." She smiled slightly. "Amelia would have approved, too, I think."

Joshua didn't answer that. But he did hope in his heart

that she would have liked the idea. He never knew what Amelia thought. He sighed a little and went on eating and chatting. He told his mother about the newest plays at the Paramount Theater and the concert that the London Symphony had given. And, especially, he told her about "SWAN LAKE" the ballet they both loved. All in all, it was a delightful time and he enjoyed every minute of it.

That night Joshua went to sleep with no dreams at all, only a lovely face that kept coming through to haunt him—dark laughing eyes, a pixie mouth and long dark, shining hair.

Back in London, several days later, he was in the therapy room at the hospital when Dr. Charles walked in. He had been struggling with the treadmill and he was getting irritated that his left leg wouldn't respond. He just stood there, holding on to the bar. He had almost decided to reach for the wheelchair when he saw her. He smiled, let go of the treadmill bar, and then he took another step. She held out her hands and he took one more step. But the strain was too much. He fell down. He was elated! He had moved! He knew it! He couldn't believe it! He had walked! For the first time in many years he had actually walked. He was laughing and crying, all at once. She helped him into the wheelchair. She was laughing with him.

"You must calm down now, Mr. Logan. You will hurt yourself. Your legs are very weak now. Every step now must be very slow. You have to get your muscles back." She leaned over and gave him a hug suddenly. "I'm so proud of you, Josh." She whispered in his ear. Then she quickly went out of the room.

He sat there awestruck. Now why had she done that? Must have been the excitement of the moment, he thought. Well, now I know I can do it. I can walk again. He sat there savoring the moment. Then he decided he was tired and hungry. He wheeled himself down to the cafeteria and bought a sandwich and a cup of coffee. He was ravenous. The sandwich went down in two bites. The coffee was hot so he only sipped it. The exhilaration was dying down. He gave some thought to the plan he had decided to do. It had to work! Just no other way! The cup of coffee was almost finished. He put it down on the table and wheeled himself around and out to the elevator. He went up the three floors to Dr. Charles office. He was hoping she would be there. He had to talk to her. There was no one else he really wanted to confide in.

He knocked on the open door. "Dr. Charles?" he called softly. "May I come in?"

Nadia looked up from her reading. She smiled quickly when she saw who it was.

"Of course, Mr. Logan. Do come in." She closed the file she was holding. "I am just finishing up this report." She put the file down on the desk and rose from her big chair. She went to the sofa by the bookcases and sat down. She said cordially, "Come, sit over here by me, Mr. Logan. I'd love to talk with you."

Joshua wheeled himself over to the sofa and stopped in front of her. "Why don't you just call me Josh?" he looked at her intently. "Dr. Charles?" He leaned over to her, very serious. "I have something I want to discuss with you. It will be easier if we are on a first name basis. All right with you?"

She stared at him, puzzled. "I think that would be fine with me, Josh."

Josh went on, "This is a very private matter, you understand?" He waited anxiously for her answer.

"All right, Mr. Lo—Josh. You may call me Nadia, then." She answered slowly. "What is the problem? Something to do with your therapy?" She was curious about his being so quiet. He was really being secretive. "I certainly hope not. You are doing marvelously well." Josh grinned at that last statement. He was well aware of his phenomenal progress in therapy.

"No, Nadia. This is a personal matter. As you know, I am the president of Grantwood-Logan Bank, and as such, I have a tremendous amount of pressure on me to conduct the bank as honestly and dignified as I can." He paused briefly, then went on. "Over the years, I have felt that I have succeeded rather well. As you probably have heard on the TV or read in the tabloids, we are considered the second largest bank in London." He took a small breath. "And the third largest bank in the international circles."

He paused again to catch his breath and gather his thoughts. Nadia nodded as she waited for him to go on. "Up to now, everything has been fine. We passed the audits and our loan package is solvent. Now, here is the problem. The other night, when I did the monthly audit, the books didn't match the cash in the vault. I recounted the cash in the vault and came up one million dollars short." He almost shouted in his anger, but he kept his voice down. "It's missing! Gone! I want to go to the police, but I need to get proof that the person I suspect is guilty." He stopped. "Do you follow me, Nadia?" He waited for her to answer, holding her hand that he had grabbed while he was talking.

She sat on the end of the sofa listening intently to every word. She thought of all the ramifications of his problem. She didn't hesitate for an instant. "Oh yes, Josh. I understand perfectly. What do you want me to do?" she squeezed the hand holding hers.

Josh felt the tiny pressure and smiled. "It won't be easy but I want you to become friends with a Mrs. Mary Lattimore. I have been invited to a party at their home tomorrow evening. I would like you to accompany me. I will introduce you to her so that she will not suspect anything. As a matter of fact, she will be delighted to see that I have a date." He laughed at that. He was very anxious, "Will you come?" He was worried that Nadia would refuse.

Nadia sat quietly for a few moments taking this conversation all in.

"I know this is slightly unusual, Nadia. But I do want you to accept my invitation." He put on his most gracious smile. She couldn't say no.

"Of course, I'll come." She laughed merrily. "It sounds like fun! It will do me good to get away from here for a while. I've always wanted to see how the other half lives."

She saw him visibly relax when she said that. She looked at her watch. It was very late for him. He must have his rest. He looks so tired. She wanted to hug him. But he wouldn't understand. Not yet.

Josh was very tired, but he was, also, very happy. It was going to work. Nadia would help him to succeed with his plan. "I'll pick you up at seven sharp tomorrow night." He said, quickly releasing her hand now.

Nadia nodded yes. The phone rang just then and she got up to answer it.

"Hello, Dr. Charles here." She said into the mouthpiece. After listening a moment, she answered, "I'll tell him. Goodbye." She hung up, grinning. "Jameson says he's waiting for you in the lobby, Josh. It's time for you to go home and I agree."

She stood up as he wheeled himself around to face the door. "Don't worry, Josh. Everything will work out, I promise. I'll see you tomorrow evening at seven sharp!" She went with him to the elevator. She pushed the elevator door open and he wheeled himself in. The door was closing, but she caught a glimpse of his smile at her as the door closed. She watched as the elevator went down.

The noises of the third floor were subdued. Nadia saw that it was past the visiting hour and her patients were beginning to go to sleep. She walked past the nurses' station to the stairs. She went down to the second floor and looked in on her young AIDS patient. He was sleeping fitfully, but seemed all right for now. She looked at his chart. She wanted to see the treatment Dr. Stives had prescribed. The medicine was not what she wanted the young man to have. Nadia decided to have a talk with the Doctor in the morning. The young man should have the new medicine now. It just might help him for a while. She would ask Dr. Stives why he hadn't prescribed it. Stepping back out into the corridor, Nadia went down the stairs to the lobby. Nurse Jacobs was at the main night desk. She looked up as Nadia went by.

"I'm heading home, Nancy. Hold down the fort!" Nadia called as she went out past the main night desk to the big front doors." I would like you to check in on the young man with "AIDS" I don't think he has been given the correct medicine."

Nurse Jacobs waved her on. "All right, Dr. Charles. Consider it done. If anything happens during the night, I will call you. I'll handle every thing here. Goodbye now. See you in the morning." She thought Nadia really looked tired. She works so hard. She's always here. Nurse Jacobs shook her head a little and wished, deep down, that she was so dedicated.

Nadia walked out to her car. The parking lot was full of fluffy, white snow and deserted. It had snowed earlier this year. As she got in and warmed up the car, she thought back to another time, another place of fluffy, white snow, and five little cold noses nuzzling her, gladly pulling her sled, rolling in that snow with her, keeping her warm when she stopped playing.

"Oh, Nefra, I do miss you, old friend." She whispered to herself. "I am coming home for Christmas. Then you and I are going to have a good run again. I will take all of you out again. I know Pookie, Pal, Nanuk, and Lucky want to run with you again."

I can hardly wait she thought as she put her hands on the wheel and backed out of the parking lot. She started to think about what Josh had told her. She would help all she could. She would do anything to catch that awful man. She knew as soon as Josh said he had a feeling he knew who had done the robbery who he was talking about. She would help get Josh's money back. She began wondering just how she would manage it.

The snow was coming down in great big flakes now. Nadia was glad the street was deserted. She pulled up to a curb and parked. She got out her door key. She ran up the stairs to the top landing and let herself into her apartment.

The little apartment was tastefully furnished with the knickknacks she brought from her home in Fairbanks that she dearly loved. Uncle Lazlo had made many little curios for her. She touched each one as she walked through the living room to her small bedroom. She smiled, as always, when she saw the beautiful quilt the ladies had made and given her for her journey to this strange country, England.

As she lay there in her bed waiting for sleep to come, Josh's face floated before her, his glistening dark eyes looking at her just like before. She smiled her little smile and closed her eyes. He would remember someday. She hoped it would be soon.

CHAPTER 9

THE PLAN CONTINUES: NOVEMBER 1986

There are always special events in every holiday season. In London it was no different. One of the most special events was "The Queen's Ball" which all the wealthy families of English society were invited to. Then there was the "Society Bazaar." This was a big auction that everyone donated to and everyone attended, rich and poor, alike. But, if you were anyone at all in English society, you definitely did not miss "The Lattimore Soiree."

Mary Lattimore went out of her way to have the most lavish, most expensive, most sought after dance party imaginable. Her mansion was lighted with the most glorious lamps from France. She imported them at a time when no one else could bring in a Swiss watch. Even her wines were exquisite.

One always wondered who it was she knew in Customs, but never dared to ask. After a while everyone just took it for granted and forgot about it. They always had a lot of fun, good food, and fantastic music. Everyone loved it. Mary was the best hostess in London.

Tonight as she danced a graceful waltz in Gary's arms, she was happy and proud of her home. She smiled at her father who was talking to the American Diplomat. She looked down at her glorious white satin gown. It set off her emerald necklace perfectly. She was glad she had bought them. She pulled a little at her long, white glove as Gary shifted his arm that was holding her. They covered the bruises Gary had given her earlier. When he saw the emerald necklace and earrings, he went berserk. He was so angry he grabbed her by the arms and threw her against the wall. Then he hit her right in the face. Luckily, she only got one black eye. She covered it with heavy makeup. After he stomped from the room, she decided the marriage was over. She would see a lawyer in the morning. Then she would throw him out. This was her home. It was her money. He would never get any more money from her. She had taken it! It was hers!

Joshua had never suspected. She laughed to herself. Even her father hadn't seen! She had gotten away with it! Mary gloated. Oh, how wrong you can be when you get overconfident. Mary had forgotten that Joshua was a very intelligent man. He would not let anything get by him, especially at the bank.

The music stopped. The guests were gravitating to the delicious well-laden food tables. Mary turned from Gary to see who was being announced. When she saw Joshua in the lobby she flew across the ballroom floor to greet him. She had never really gotten over her infatuation of him. "Oh, Josh! I'm so glad to see you!" She gushed out happily and took the hand Josh held out to her. "I just knew you would come!"

She saw Nadia beside him. Mary looked her over with piercing brown eyes. "And who is this? I don't believe we've met." She shook her long, blonde hair back and waited. Nadia smiled sweetly. She was not overly impressed with this tall, blonde woman dressed in white satin.

Joshua let go of her hand and took Nadia's, smiling at her, inwardly hoping she would not be nervous. Nadia had been to a lot of hospital functions that Joshua hadn't known about. She was not a bit nervous at being here for this one. She just kept smiling.

"This is Dr. Nadia Charles, Mary." He paused for a moment. "Dr. Charles is helping me with my therapy." He hesitated, "I hope you two will be friends soon. I am hoping Nadia will enjoy being here. She has been very busy lately at the hospital." He turned to Nadia, smiling. Nadia smiled back as she put her hand on his shoulder.

"This is Mrs. Mary Lattimore," he said quietly to Nadia.

He remembered how Mary had been so affectionate when they were younger. Amelia had noticed, too.

Nadia shook Mary's hand. She smiled again. "How do you do, Mrs. Lattimore? You certainly have a most elegant home." Nadia looked around. She noticed a fur throw on one of the sofas that lined the dance floor. "I see you have a liking for Alaskan fur, too." Nadia had recognized the fur throw as one of Charlie's.

"Gary gave me that throw when we were married." Mary answered casually. "I don't know where he got it." She said nonchalantly. "He gave me lots of things over the years."

Gary came up beside them. "Come on, Josh. Let's have a drink." He wheeled Joshua toward the library doors, giving Mary his awful smile Nadia knew so well. She heard him say, "Glad you could make it, Josh. I have to talk to you privately." He ignored Nadia.

Mary had gone to greet some of her other guests. The music had started up again. People were dancing and Nadia stood for a moment watching them. Many of the men were staring at her, too. She was quite beautiful in her lavender jacquard gown with the puffed sleeves and full skirt. Around her neck she wore the amethyst and ivory necklace that Uncle Lazlo had given her for her birthday years ago. It went perfectly with her little amethyst earrings that she had found in a shop on Danbury Lane one rainy day. She knew they were for her as soon as she had seen them.

Nadia walked over to the food tables and put some food on her plate. Then she went over to the sofa and sat down on the fur throw. She put a few bites of food in her mouth and swallowed them. It was a delicious salad but she couldn't swallow any more. She put the plate down on a table next to the sofa and ran her hand across the fur throw just as she had seen Josh do with the mink coat. She was remembering when Charlie had brought this particular fur throw home. On the corner she saw the initials A.C.

All the time she was thinking how she could befriend Mary Lattimore. How could she ever find a topic to talk to her about? They had so little in common. But she had noticed the bruises on her cheek under her eye! The thick makeup was wearing off a bit. Nadia just sat a few moments more and ate a little more of her food.

Several very prominent men came up to her. One of them asked her to dance. Nadia was flattered. She was going to refuse, then she thought of all the questions Nancy would ask. What could she tell her if she didn't dance at least once! It wasn't as if she didn't know how! She had always been asked out at college. She was a good dancer. Teacher Neal had taken her to her first Prom and taught her the steps. She had loved learning to dance!

So she danced with the American diplomat who, she found out, was very much interested in her native land, Alaska. She mentioned the plans for the oil pipeline the government was planning to build. When she left Nome for school, they hadn't started on it. Nadia told the diplomat that she had read about it in the papers that Uncle Lazlo had sent her.

The American diplomat laughed and told her, "Of course, it's already finished now. It was quite a project, too." The music stopped. He led her back to the sofa. He was very gracious in his thanks for the dance. She picked up her plate and ate a few more bites. Dancing always did make her hungry!

The music started up again. A very impressive looking gentleman came toward her. "Mr. Malcolm Gregory, at your service, Ma'am. Would you have this set with me?"

Nadia looked up at him. "I would be delighted, sir." She accepted graciously as she took his outstretched hand. As they moved around the floor he told her that he was the Chief of Scotland Yard. He had wanted to meet her ever since she had come into the room.

He knew Joshua well and expressed surprise to see him here. Nadia felt comfortable in his arms as he whirled her around the floor. He had the most delightful accent she had ever heard and such a delicious sense of humor. The laughter just rolled off his tongue as he made remark after remark about the people around them. He seemed to know everyone and he didn't mind telling her about the antics. She was fascinated. She had never met anyone so charming before. She was very disappointed when the music stopped.

Malcolm thanked her, genuinely sorry that he had to be going. But, as he lightly kissed her hand, he said he would like to see her again. With a twinkle in his eye he said, " In my office tomorrow, Dr. Charles."

She looked at him speechless. Then nodded. All the way across the room she watched him as he almost marched out the door.

It was just then that Joshua and Gary came out of the library. Nadia saw that Joshua was very quiet. Gary wheeled Joshua up to the sofa where Nadia sat waiting. Even Gary had no awful smile for her. He said goodbye to them and quickly sought out Mary at the far end of the ballroom.

It was time to go. Joshua was exhausted. "Nadia, Will you find Jameson, please?"

She heard the exhaustion in his voice. She was worried. As she started toward the kitchen area past the ballroom doors, she saw Jameson bringing their coats. Some of the other guests were leaving and they joined them.

Jameson pushed Joshua to the elevator to the lower level while Nadia waited at the bottom of the great stairs out front. Jameson wheeled Joshua to the limousine and put him in. Joshua had nothing to say. When they came up to where Nadia was standing, he opened the door and she got in picking up her skirt as she shut the door. No one wanted to talk.

As they rode, Joshua made the effort to tell her what had transpired in the library. It seemed Gary wanted to borrow money from him. That was a surprise! As Gary kept talking he realized that Gary knew nothing of the missing million dollars from his vault. So, it must have been Mary or her father. He paused and looked at Nadia. She was very quiet.

Nadia said nothing. She was thinking about the events at the party. She heard Joshua's story, but she didn't know how to answer him just then. She just looked out the window at the snow.

Joshua was not certain what to do or say. Then it hit him! Of course! He had never given her a corsage! He had even forgotten to tell her how beautiful she looked. "Oh, Nadia." He said contritely as he took her hand. "I am such a clumsy oaf! You must forgive me. You were the most beautiful woman there and I never even told you! I am sorry!" He squeezed her hand gently as he smiled at her. "Please accept my apology and don't be angry with me."

"Oh, Josh, shush!" She turned and looked at him. Her dark eyes were glistening in the evening light. She leaned over and kissed him lightly on the cheek. "I will always forgive you." She whispered softly.

He reached over and held her close for a moment. It was as if time stood still. Why did this small gesture stir him so? Why did the touch of her hair against his cheek make his heart suddenly want to leap out of his chest? Why did this woman feel so natural in his arms? He couldn't answer these questions that scurried through his head. He just held her, his soul at peace within him. He smiled to himself as they sped on.

Then Jameson turned and said to them as they pulled up to the curb, "Here is your apartment, Dr. Charles."

The moment was gone. But, for Joshua, the moment was the start of feelings he hadn't felt for fifteen years. Nadia was slow to get out. But Jameson was holding the door for her so she picked up her skirt and ran for the steps. The snow quickly covered her as she stood on the landing.

As they drove home Joshua was content. He felt that he had accomplished something by hearing Gary out. He would have to think more about Mary and her father tomorrow. He watched Jameson guide the limousine down the snow-covered road. Dark eyes and shining hair surrounding a lovely little face were floating in his mind.

Nadia stood on the landing and watched the limousine go around the corner. It was out of sight immediately. The wind whipped some of the snowflakes into her face. She brushed them away with a flip of her hand.

She was feeling mixed emotions as she put the key into the lock. There was so much that had happened to her at the party. Meeting Malcolm Gregory, for instance, wondering why he would want to see her. Mary Lattimore being so nonchalant about the fur throw and what about the bruises on her face and arms? Why was she hiding them? What had happened to her? And then—there was Josh, holding her quietly, tenderly. She had always hoped that some day he would hold her like that and now it had happened. She was so ecstatic! Her heart was pounding! She took a deep breath as she felt the cold wind rustled her skirt.

She shivered as she opened the door. As she stepped into her living room, the warmth caressed her. She walked over to the big window overlooking the street below and gazed out. There was only snow coming down. She stood there, thinking.

Another winter, another time—when Uncle Lazlo told her she was going to London General. She was so excited that night! The tears were starting. She wiped them away. She turned from the window and went to the telephone. Dialing the number quieted her feelings as she waited for the rings to be answered.

"Hello, This is London General Hospital. Nurse Jacobs speaking." came the answer. "How may I help you?"

"Nancy, Dr. Charles here." Nadia said calmly "I want the status report on my AIDS patient. I gave his casework to Doctor Stives." She paused a moment. "Has he followed up on my request?" She waited for Nurse Jacobs to answer.

"Dr. Charles," Nurse Jacobs was quick to say." I have the file here on my desk. I am looking at the file now and I don't see any change in the medications as yet. Tom is sleeping fitfully, but he seems stable for the moment."

"All right, Nancy," Nadia answered. "Do look in on him during your shift, please. Notify me of any changes. I'm going to bed now." She hung up. She will talk to Dr. Stives in the morning. She was not happy to hear what Nurse Jacobs told her.

Nurse Jacobs put down the telephone and went on her rounds. Too bad Dr. Stives wasn't at the hospital just then. She knew Nadia was upset. She went down the corridor to Room 12 and looked in. Tom was still sleeping, but he was not moving back and forth. He was lying on his side quietly. Nurse Jacobs closed the door and went down the corridor to her other patients.

As Nadia climbed into bed, she let her mind go back to the ride home. She was thinking that perhaps Josh was starting to remember more. The wind rattled the shutters as she closed her eyes and slept.

All in all, it had been a very memorable night.

CHAPTER 10

INTERRUPTIONS: NOVEMBER 1986

The next morning Nadia arrived at London General early. She wanted to catch Dr. Stives before he went off duty. She spotted him coming down the corridor.

"Hello, Dr. Charles. You're here very early this morning." He greeted her pleasantly.

"Yes, I am, Dr. Stives." Nadia was not anxious to begin this talk. "I have something I want to talk to you about." She took his arm as they walked down the corridor. "Let's have some breakfast and chat. I could use a good cup of coffee."

At the cafeteria she ordered toast and coffee for both of them. As they carried their trays to one of the tables, Nadia sat down with Dr. Stives sitting down opposite her, waiting. He could sense that she was a little agitated. "I referred a young man to you the other day. I noticed in his file that you have not prescribed the new medicine for him yet. Why is that?" She asked, sipping her coffee.

"Well." Dr. Stives hesitated. "I just didn't think it would be right for him at this time. He doesn't have long to live, as far as I can tell."

Dr. Stives was certainly frank she thought. "I see." Nadia was adamant. "I want you to have him on the new medicine by this afternoon. Her voice took on an angry tone. "We are here to help him live as long as he can, Dr. Stives. Not to watch him die!" her voice was getting angrier. "Do I make myself clear?" She stood up and looked at her watch. "I have to make my rounds now. If you have any questions about this treatment, I will be in my office later."

Dr. Stives was stunned, but he managed to answer her respectfully. "Yes, Ma'am." After all, she was the Administrator. She was responsible for the completion of his internship. "I'll take care of it immediately."

"Good." Nadia smiled at him graciously, realizing how stern she must have sounded. She hated to be so direct with her interns but sometimes they were just too unfeeling. She shook her head slightly. Dr. Stives was a good intern. Just young. Like the man he was caring for.

Nadia passed the front desk. She told Nurse Jacobs she would be gone a couple of hours and to hold her calls. She went out to her car in the parking lot and got in. She was thinking about Chief Inspector Gregory. Malcolm!

As she drove down the avenue past Hyde Park and Buckingham Palace, the Queen's home, she marveled that a young lady from Nome, Alaska could be here in a big hospital in London, England. Such beautiful sights! Uncle Lazlo will be so surprised to hear her stories.

She wondered what Chief Inspector Gregory wanted to talk to her about. Perhaps it was the situation at Josh's bank.

Nadia drove down the River Thames road watching as the people struggled to brave the windy, snowy walkway.

The Scotland Yard towers loomed up ahead of her. The red brick glittered in the winter sun. She drove through the gate into the courtyard and parked.

As Nadia walked into the beautiful rotunda of Scotland Yard, she was in awe of its size.

She looked around for the elevators and saw them on each side of her. Chief Inspector Gregory's office was on the third floor. Her mind was in a whirl as she rode up in the elevator to his floor.

Chief Inspector Gregory was reading a paper as she was ushered in. He motioned for her to sit down in the big leather chair. Again she was impressed by his manner.

She waited, watching him curiously as he finished reading the paper and laid it down on his desk. "Hello, Dr. Charles." He said cordially. "I am delighted to see you again. I am glad you could make it." He grinned slightly. "I suppose you are wondering why this summons?"

Nadia hesitated a moment, cautiously answering. "Yes, I am."

Chief Inspector Gregory picked up the paper again. He paused slightly, "I have a report here from the Police Department of Fairbanks, Alaska notifying me of a murder and a theft."

Nadia was shocked. She had never realized the police in Fairbanks would keep the case open. Uncle Lazlo must have requested it.

Chief Inspector Gregory went on. "Two people were found murdered and a number of furs were stolen. It seems this tragedy happened several years ago. They never closed the case. They were asking us if we could help them in any way. So any information we can give them, they would be grateful for. I heard you mention at the party last night that you were from Alaska. I want to ask you if you know anything about this tragic happening." Chief Inspector Gregory's voice droned in her ears, but Nadia was not listening. All she could see was Charlie and Annie lying in a pool of blood and that awful man laughing.

"Dr. Charles, did you hear me?" Chief Inspector Gregory was saying quietly.

Nadia looked at him. "Oh, yes, Chief Inspector Gregory. I heard you," She sat up and moved forward in the chair. "I have waited years for this to come to light. I will be glad to tell you all about it." She went on. "Those people were my foster parents. The stolen furs belonged to them. Charlie had made them for selling in Anchorage so I could go to school. But some awful men stole them and killed Charlie and Annie. They never saw me! But I saw one of them! The murderer!" She was screaming, crying.

Anger and pain and the frustration all came out as she spoke. The tears and grief of eighteen years finally came to the fore as little Starflower (Nadia) cried. Chief Inspector Gregory got up and walked around his desk to take her in his arms. "Oh, my God!" He breathed as he held her close. "How could you have held this grief in for all these years?" He patted her shoulder as he tried to comfort her.

Starflower (Nadia) gulped down her tears, realizing she was a grown woman now. She was beginning to be embarrassed by her outburst. "I'm sorry, Chief Inspector Gregory. I don't usually give way like that." She hid her face in the handkerchief he had given her.

"Do you know this man?" Chief Inspector Gregory asked quickly, feeling that he knew the answer.

"Gary Lattimore did it." The relief was evident in her voice. "I recognized him when he came to my office some days ago. He came to see Amelia Logan who was killed in a car accident.. I didn't know what to do, so I just waited. You have answered my prayers. I thank you so much."

She was comforted when she felt the gentle pressure of

his arms around her shoulders. But she had mixed emotions as she held his hand. She started to back away—looking at him quizzically as she did so. He had forgotten that he was still holding her. He saw her look and swiftly let her go.

Again Nadia looked at him. He was a very impressive figure standing at his desk. She started to leave, hesitated. Something told her to tell him about the situation at Josh's bank.

Then she decided Josh should tell him so she suggested that Chief Inspector Gregory come to see Josh in the therapy room at the hospital. Chief Inspector Gregory smiled. Then he told her to be very careful when dealing with the Lattimores. He didn't want her to be hurt.

If Gary Lattimore ever found out that she knew him and what he had done in Fort Yukon, her life would be in grave danger.

"He knows nothing of me." She scoffed. "I have to get back to my office and my patients. She looked at him. "See you at lunch?"

"Yes, of course, Dr. Charles," he answered quickly. "Lunch at noon. See you then." He smiled at her again as she turned to leave. Chief Inspector Gregory watched her as she went out the door. She turned, waved, and was gone.

He sat at his desk, thinking hard. He really hated to see her go. He picked up the paper again, trying to concentrate on the job at hand. But a beautiful face with glistening brown eyes kept floating in front of him, blinding him to the print on the paper. As he had seen at the dance, she was a lovely young woman. Her patience and strength in handling her grief had stirred a cord in him.

Nadia hesitated for a moment at the top of the stairs. No, she had no right to be thinking those thoughts. She had enough on her mind with the news from Alaska. She ran down the stairs, through the long rotunda to her car.

He wanted to see her again. He reminded himself that he was going to see her at lunch in a few hours. Suddenly, he started smiling. "Ramsey." He called through the intercom. "Get in here now."

"Yes sir!" Ramsey said as he came through the door. Chief Inspector Gregory handed him the report from Fairbanks. "We've got a murderer to catch. Answer this immediately!" Ramsey reached out and took the report.

"Tell them we have their man!" Chief Inspector Gregory went on. "He isn't in our custody yet, but it won't be long. They can send someone over anytime they want. Just have them notify me when they arrive."

"Right, Chief. I'm on my way," Ramsey was out the door as fast as 200 pounds would move. He was a big man with a heart of gold.

Chief Inspector Gregory was still smiling after him. He walked over to the window. The parking lot below was clear. The early morning snow had melted. He went back to his desk and picked up some files. Then he grabbed his jacket from the closet and strode out of the office. He dropped the files down on Ramsey's desk. "Take care of these." He yelled. "I'll be back soon."

Ramsey nodded his head and smiled. The Chief was always in a hurry.

Chief Inspector Gregory marveled at the children playing in the schoolyard as he drove by. Perhaps he would go up to Northhampton one of these days and see his son. It must be five years now. Mabel couldn't be angry now. He hoped not. Perhaps he would go up for Christmas this year. Ian would like that. Chief Inspector Gregory grinned. I would like that!

London General loomed large in the distance. He brought his mind back to the problem at hand. The snow had started to fall again as he pulled into the almost full parking lot. He found a discreet spot on the outer curb and put the police car he was driving into it. He got out and walked through the parking lot to the lobby of the hospital. It was becoming cold again. He pulled up his collar as he went, shivering all the way. He was lucky. The lobby was warm.

Chief Inspector Gregory walked up the stairs to the front desk where Nurse Jacobs was standing with the telephone in her hand. She saw him coming as she said into the telephone. "I'll send him along, Dr. Charles." She put down the telephone.

Nurse Jacobs pointed him the way down the corridor to the Therapy Room. Chief Inspector Gregory looked into the room. He saw Dr. Charles standing there. He also saw a very angry man in a wheelchair struggling to get up from it. He surmised that this angry man was Joshua Logan. He certainly didn't look like the powerful banker today. He was trying to move his legs, but it just wasn't to be. He just sat there in his wheelchair, clenching his fists, not speaking. The frustration in his face was evident.

Nadia put down the file she was holding and walked over to him. "Don't struggle so." She said calmly. "It will become easier soon. You must give your muscles a chance."

She was leaning over to adjust his chair to a more comfortable position, patting his hand as she straightened up. The gesture was faintly familiar. Joshua looked up at her. How strange!

She was speaking again. "You know, it's been eighteen years! Of course, you will be weak." Josh just groaned.

She saw Malcolm standing in the doorway, watching. She made a motion to him to come in. She touched Josh's hair gently as she walked past him. Josh looked up at her again. He sensed something in that touch! Then he saw Malcolm walking up toward him. The thought fled.

"Here is someone I want you to meet." Nadia said, looking

down at Joshua. "This is Chief Inspector Gregory of Scotland Yard."

She took Malcolm's hand and brought him closer to Joshua. "This is my friend and patient, Mr. Joshua Logan of Grantwood—Logan Bank, Limited."

Joshua held out his hand as Nadia made the introduction quickly. "How do you do, Chief Inspector Gregory?" he said graciously. "Delighted to meet you."

Malcolm took his hand. "Dr. Charles mentioned you wanted to talk to me." He waited quietly. Joshua didn't answer. He asked patiently again, "What is your problem, Mr. Logan?"

Joshua wasn't sure he wanted to talk about it now. He looked at Nadia, then again at Malcolm.

"Care to tell me if it concerns the bank?" Malcolm persisted patiently again.

Josh spoke indignantly. "I was trying to work it out by myself." He paused, looking very sheepish. "I guess I could use your help, Chief Inspector Gregory." Josh looked over at Nadia standing next to him and smiled. "My plan was to find out if Mrs. Lattimore would tell Dr. Charles about any new purchases she made in the last few months! I'm almost certain she has, somehow, stolen a million dollars from my bank."

Nadia mentioned again that she had nothing in common with Mrs. Lattimore. She had never met her before last night. She looked over at Josh. She said she would help if she could.

Joshua wanted her to become friends with Mrs. Lattimore.

Malcolm was astonished. Didn't she know the danger? Didn't Joshua realize? He looked at Nadia standing next to Joshua, concern showing in her eyes. She shook her head at Malcolm. Joshua knew nothing of her relationship with the Lattimores. She didn't want him to know. Malcolm understood.

Nurse Jacobs came to the door just then. "Emergency! You're needed in surgery, Dr. Charles."

Nadia breathed a sigh of relief. "I'm on my way." She ran down the corridor to the "ER"

Nurse Jacobs was right behind her. "Is the baby coming out normally?" Nadia yelled at Nurse Jacobs. She never saw Nurse Jacobs shake her head NO. For the next seven hours Nadia was very busy. Delivering a baby that was breach took all her concentration. She forgot all about the Lattimores, Joshua, and Chief Inspector Gregory.

The door swished shut behind them. The bright winter sun warmed the tiles of the Therapy Room. The silence surrounded the two men like a blanket. Chief Inspector Gregory stood still and watched as Joshua wheeled his chair over to the treadmill. He had a feeling he knew what Joshua was trying to do.

Joshua wanted to stand again. The way he did on Queen Charlotte Island on his mother's porch. He put his hands on the bar and tried to pull himself up. "I will do this." He said to no one in particular. Then he realized Chief Inspector Gregory was watching. "Sorry. I forgot for a moment that you were here." He stood up very slowly. His legs were so weak! He turned and looked at Chief Inspector Gregory. "I did it!" He exclaimed. "Soon I will walk!" He felt himself falling and sat down in his wheelchair again. He motioned to Chief Inspector Gregory to help him to the table at the far end of the room. Malcolm took the handles of the wheelchair and pushed him across the floor all the while saying, "Joshua, please call me Malcolm. It would make it easier for us to understand what we must do to solve your problem, don't you think?"

Joshua agreed. "All right, Malcolm it is!"

Nurse Jacobs came through the door with a tray of tea and sandwiches. She put the tray down on the table. "Dr. Charles thought you two should have some nourishment." She smiled. "Dr. Charles is tied up in surgery now, but she will see you both when she is finished with her patient." She looked at Joshua sitting there quietly. She thought he looked a little tired.

Joshua thanked her. "We will be a couple of hours ourselves." He turned to Malcolm. "We have to talk about a few things."

Nurse Jacobs smiled at him and left. The door swished after her. The telephone at the front reception desk was ringing.

Malcolm poured their tea as he said, "I can't allow you to involve Dr. Charles in your plan, Joshua. Don't you know how treacherous these people are? Her life could be in grave danger."

"Yes. Malcolm. I do know these people very well. I can't think of any other way to catch them." Joshua thought a moment. Then he asked Malcolm a question. "Do you have a plan?"

Joshua was serious. He was reasonably sure that Malcolm didn't have a specific plan thought out, either. He waited for an answer from Malcolm.

Knowing Nadia's complete involvement in this situation made it difficult for Malcolm to comment. But he said, "If you can make sure Dr. Charles won't be hurt in any way, I guess I can go along with your plan for now."

Joshua looked at him, curious at his words, but glad he had accepted it. He reassured Malcolm that Nadia would be fine. He could hardly wait to tell Nadia. He did wonder what Malcolm had meant. How could Nadia be in danger? Since they were in complete agreement, they finished their tea and sandwiches.

Malcolm got up and pushed Joshua to the door. The door swished open and the two men went down the corridor to the front desk where Nurse Jacobs was holding the telephone. "Dr. Charles is on her way, Gentlemen." She said as she put down the telephone.

She came around the corner of the desk and walked up to Joshua. She took his pulse as she always did when he finished a session in the Therapy Room. She noticed that he was breathing a little hard. "You must take a rest, Mr. Logan. Dr. Charles would not like it if I let you collapse."

Joshua told her he was feeling a little tired, but it was nothing to worry about. He assured her he would rest when he got home. He didn't want Dr. Charles to stop his exercises. He felt that he was coming along very well. In the back of his mind he knew someday he would walk again!

"Keep me posted, Joshua." Malcolm patted Joshua's shoulder. He walked out the big front doors to his car. He drove up the road to his office at Scotland Yard. Ramsey would have a lot of news for him when he got there. He mulled over the plan Joshua outlined for him. He hoped that Dr. Charles would not run into any trouble. Snow was falling intermittently. He loved the dusk in London. The shadows reminded him of his home on the moors. He smiled when he saw the towers of the great edifice that was Scotland Yard looming in the distance.

Joshua sat quietly waiting for Nadia to come down the corridor. As he watched he saw the dark, shining hair and the big brown eyes gleaming at him from under the white cap doctors wear in surgery. He felt a twinge in his heart when she reached up and took it off. The gesture seemed so familiar. Where had he seen it before?

"Well, Josh." She said. "How did your talk with Chief Inspector Gregory go?" She grinned at him. "Did he like your plan?"

"He wasn't too enthused about it. But he did say it was all right." Joshua answered her. He looked up at her grinning face. "Oh, Nadia, I know it will work. I sensed something was wrong with Mary Lattimore last night." He shrugged. "We'll soon find out, won't we?"

Nadia nodded her head yes. She had the same feeling, too.

Just then, Jameson came in the door. "It's time to go, Mr. Logan." He took the handles of the wheelchair and swung Joshua around to the elevators. The limousine was on the lower floor. As the elevators swished open, Joshua turned to wave to Nadia standing in the doorway. She tingled as she remembered another wave, another time. She watched as they drove away.

Jameson drove the limousine smoothly through the light snow as they sped off down the road to home. Joshua's townhouse was on the other side of town from Scotland Yard. It was a long ride. He spent the time thinking about his plan. He was happy that Nadia said she would help. He was content now that things would work out. He also kept thinking about the twinge in his heart.

CHAPTER 11

THE ATTEMPT: DECEMBER 1986

The Lattimore Soiree' was a great success. Mary was delighted as she sat admiring her emeralds in the vanity mirror. They set off her green speckled eyes so that even in the dim light of her bedroom they just gleamed. She thought about that charming Prime Minister who was such a comedian when he wasn't around his austere wife. They had laughed and laughed as they danced. And that other gentleman! The American Diplomat! He had the most unusual accent! He was so interested in that old fur throw! She frowned in the mirror.

He knew it was from Alaska, too. It seemed he knew a lot about Alaska. So did Nadia Charles. The doctor. He had told her Dr. Charles was from Alaska—a funny little town called Nome. She wondered where that was! She would have to ask Gary. He had given it to her when he asked her to marry him. She frowned again.

That old fur! She really didn't like it very much. She

always thought it was too old! She didn't like Gary not telling her about it either. She had known Gary came from Anchorage in Alaska with her father. Gary had told her that much a long time ago. Her father wouldn't talk about it at all!

She had been fascinated when her father broke his silence. He told her about the mountains. And the snow! More snow than London ever got! All London ever got was pea soup fog and cold, wet streets in the fall. The winter snow was worse! Just plain slushy snow most of the time! And always, so cold and windy! She hated it!

In fact, it was cold right now. Mary shivered even though her bedroom was warm. She looked around her elegant bedroom. She loved the dark blue drapes at the windows. The dark blue bedspread—custom made—was a perfect match for her big bed. She shopped for hours looking for the carpet. She found just the one from India. A gorgeous blue-flowered creation she fell in love with the minute she saw it in the store.

She smiled, reaching up to release her hair. It fell in golden ringlets around her shoulders, cascading down her back. She shook her head to make sure it was loose. In the mirror she saw Gary standing behind her.

His face was distorted, his mood angry.

She didn't want to see him like this. He always ended up hitting her. Gleaming emeralds in the dim light caught his eye. "Take off those damn emeralds." He growled. "You knew I didn't want you buying them now. You knew I needed the money for my new venture." He was livid! "You spent it deliberately on those frivolous jewels."

He walked quickly over to her and made a grab for them. She jerked away and ran for the door. The door wouldn't open. She pulled on it. It was locked! It took her a moment to realize she was trapped. She had to try another tactic. He was coming at her with his fists clenched and murder in his eyes. She ran back to the vanity and sat down.

"What do you know about Alaska?' She paused. "Where did you get that old throw?" She went on, hoping to stop his angry outbursts. " Gary, Nadia Charles told me it came from Fort Yukon. And so did you. When I first met you." She stopped, breathless. And waited.

Her words stopped him cold. He just stared at her, eyes glistening angrily. He burst out belligerently. "You know I went to Alaska in 1968 with your father. We had some business in Anchorage." He went on, the angry tone gone from his voice. "We were trying to save the bank."

Mary waited and listened. She certainly did remember that awful day! The people were so upset they were screaming to have their money back! Gary was not there. She had to be calm.

Gary was explaining, "We went for a drive up around Fort Yukon. We stopped in at this little Native store up there." He started to shout, "I bought the furs! I told you. I bought the furs!" He watched her face—it never changed expression. He went on. "Your father wrote you about it when you were at that boarding school in Switzerland."

She looked at him in wonder. She had never gotten any letters from her father—at school or anytime since. She would have to ask him about the letter Gary was talking about. Strange, very strange!

She became very calm. She had to get him to open the door. She put her hand on her hair to push it back and took a deep breath. It was only a moment, but it seemed like a lifetime. She knew what she had to do.

"Gary, I want you to open the door. Locking me in won't help you." She waited for him to move back to the door. She took another deep breath. "I have something I want to tell you. I have decided to get a divorce. I will be seeing a lawyer in the morning." She turned back to the mirror. "Now, goodnight." Did he hear her? She had wanted to shock him. She saw that her words had stung him. He was dumbfounded!

She looked at him through the mirror as she unhooked the emeralds and laid them on the vanity. She reached up and took off the earrings. She laid them next to the necklace. She held her breath and just sat there quietly. If he were going to hit her, now would be the time.

He wanted to grab her, throw her against the wall. Maybe, even choke her. But he didn't. Not this time. He unlocked the door and stalked through, slamming it after himself as he quickly walked down the hall. In his room he thought, "I'll kill her. I swear I will!" He decided he was hungry. He went down to the kitchen, muttering all the way. "I'll find a way, somehow. She's not going to do this to me. She can't!" He stood there, fists clenched.

Divorce was out of the question! As long as Mary was his wife, he could always con her out of some money. He knew she had a lot more than she let on to him. Ever since she left the bank! He was always getting her to sign for him. She paid his bills and never even looked at them. He just then came up with a thought. He would write out the release form on her bank account. She would sign it and never even know she was giving it to him. Ingenious! He chuckled at his idea. He had made her sign several forms that were in her desk.

Already he felt better. He ate the cookie that was lying on the counter and drank his cup of coffee as he thought of how he would spend all her money. He would have to take care of her father, too. He thought her father was the reason she talked about divorce. He always wondered what her father had written in that letter. Gary shook his head slightly, thinking.

He could never find it, either. He had looked everywhere for it after he and Mary came home from the honeymoon. Gary ate another cookie out of the bag. He was afraid that Mary's father had weakened. The years always took their toll. Robert was getting old now. Robert could go to the police anytime, tomorrow, next week, or next month. Gary couldn't chance it. Robert would have to go.

Later that night, Nadia was at her desk in the "Inner Sanctum" when the telephone rang. The voice at the other end was very faint. "Dr. Charles? Please—help—me. He—has—poisoned—me. I'm—Mary—Latti–more." The telephone went dead.

Nadia was stunned. She hung up the telephone. She pushed the button on the intercom to summon the ambulance to the parking lot. Then she pushed another button and gave the ambulance driver the address of the Lattimore mansion. She heard the sirens as they left.

She picked up the telephone again and called the front desk. Nurse Abrams answered after a moment. "Hello. This is the front desk, Nurse Abrams speaking."

"Janet, get "ER" ready, stat! We're going to be busy in a few minutes. Poison case coming in!" Nadia spoke quickly. "Hurry!"

Nurse Abrams responded just as quickly. "Okay, Dr. Charles. I'm on my way!" She took off running down the corridor.

Fifteen minutes later the ambulance backed up to the double doors and the paramedics wheeled Mary Lattimore in. She was unconscious, but alive. Nadia took one look at her and motioned for Janet to pump out her stomach. They worked steadily until Mary opened her eyes and started breathing, slowly, regularly. Nurse Abrams cleaned up.

Nadia went back out into the corridor. "You boys are a wonder! We have been able to save her, thanks to your quick response!"

The Paramedics grinned, "Thanks, Doc." Their night was just beginning. They appreciated the compliment. It didn't happen often.

Much later, Mary was sleeping comfortably and she had sent Janet home. It had been a busy night again. Nadia sat back in her big leather chair, thinking. A train accident had taken up much of her time in "ER" right after Mrs. Lattimore had been seen to. She was tired, but satisfied. Now she would know how to talk to Mrs. Lattimore. She would get to the bottom of things! She was almost asleep when she heard the sound of footsteps in the corridor.

Chief Inspector Gregory walked into Nadia's office. He sat down in the other big leather chair. He looked at her. He could see she was showing the strain of the earlier ordeal with Mary Lattimore. She didn't want to talk to him at that moment. She said nothing. She waited for him to speak.

"You look tired out, Dr. Charles. I heard you had a busy time tonight." He waited for her to answer. She didn't. He frowned and went on. "I, too, had a bit of success. I talked to your friend, Mr. Logan. He had quite a little story to tell me. He has come up with a plan that involves you." He hesitated, hoping she would refuse to be a part of the crazy plan. "Are you really going through with it?"

"Yes, Malcolm." Nadia finally answered. "I am going to talk to Mrs. Lattimore later." Nadia was irritated with his question because she had already told him the same thing in the Therapy Room.

Chief Inspector Gregory sighed and got up from the big leather chair. He walked over to the window. By the tone of her voice, he knew he couldn't stop her. "Then I want you to be careful of what you say. Especially around her husband!"

Nadia shook her head. She understood what he meant. She was well aware of the situation.

Chief Inspector Gregory walked back to the big leather chair. He sat down again. He started to speak again, more seriously. "I must tell you, Dr. Charles, that we have learned that he is responsible for his wife being here." He went on to explain. "The maid told us this morning that she found the glass of poisoned milk. He had given her the milk and cookies just before she went to bed." He paused. He saw Nadia nodding off. She was trying to stay awake.

"We checked it out." He saw Nadia close her eyes for a moment. "I'll hurry this up. We don't want to give anything away about the Alaskan investigation. We need more proof." He took a breath and went on. "And, we need proof that the Lattimores are involved in the disappearance of Mr. Logan's money." She was falling asleep! "I won't spoil anything for you, Malcolm. I want to know everything as much as you do." She yawned and stood up from her big leather chair, hand out. "It's been a long night." She yawned again. " Good night, Malcolm."

Chief Inspector Gregory smiled when he heard her say his name. He took the hand she had out, shook it gently, and backed to the door. "Call me later. Please?" He said as he went out, closing the door.

Nadia heard the elevator whirr on its downward descent. She yawned again as she looked at her watch. Three o'clock a.m.! Her day would begin in two hours. She lay down on the sofa at the far end of her office. She was asleep in minutes.

Later that evening, Nadia stopped in to see Mary Lattimore. She was resting quietly. Nadia checked her chart and saw that her prognosis was good. But Nadia knew any agitation at this point would prove devastating to her patient.

Mary was looking out over the rooftops of London, her blond ringlets surrounding her face like a golden halo. Her brown-green-speckled eyes were sad. She was trying to find words to tell Doctor Charles her story. She turned toward Nadia, weakly lifting a hand to her. "Dr. Charles, I have to tell you what happened." Mary was surprised how easy it was to talk to Nadia.

"Mrs. Lattimore, please, don't excite yourself now." Nadia was very concerned. Her patient could go into shock any time. "You had a rough night. You are still weak. You must rest." Nadia couldn't help sounding anxious.

"I feel fine, Dr. Charles. Please listen to me." Mary was determined to speak. Her voice was getting stronger. "I must tell someone or I shall go crazy. I know my husband did this to me. He was so angry the night of the party. I had no idea he wanted to kill me!" Mary's eyes filled with tears.

The agitation Nadia was worried about was only moments away. She could see the anxiety coming through. Mary's hands were clasping and unclasping on the blanket. Her eyes were red with tears. But she continued. "He wanted the emeralds so much! You saw them, didn't you? Dr. Charles?" She looked up at Nadia from her pillow. "Weren't they lovely?"

Nadia smiled as she sat down by the bed and held Mary's hands. The small gesture seemed to calm her. Nadia nodded her head. "Yes, they were magnificent. You must cherish them."

Mary smiled back slightly. "I put them in the safe when I went to bed. Gary doesn't know the combination. I never told him." She blinked back more tears. The brown-green-speckled eyes were red now. She went on. "I never knew the milk was poisoned!" She hesitated, then said quietly, "I always have milk and cookies before I go to bed. I am glad now that I didn't drink it all like I usually do." She stopped talking, sighed a little and looked back out the window. The snow of the December night was coming down in big flakes that were covering the roofs with a blanket of white. Mary was squeezing Nadia's hand tightly, afraid to let go.

"Dr. Charles," She started again. "You know about Alaska! I know that because Mr. Acorn told me when we were dancing. He was the American Diplomat who also danced with you!"

Nadia gasped!

Mary didn't wait for Nadia to answer. "Do you know the Fort Yukon Territory?" She was breathing heavily; words were just coming out. "My father and Gary were there many years ago. Did you know my father wrote about it?" She paused, her voice weakening. "But I never got the letter. Gary told me father wrote it after they made a trip to that territory. I wonder what my father did with it?" She looked hard into Nadia's eyes as she asked the next question. "I wonder, why hasn't my father come to see me?" Her tears started to flow again.

Nadia was flabbergasted at this question. She had no idea Mary's father hadn't come to visit. She had been so busy. She hadn't noticed! She had been aware of the milk and cookies incident. Malcolm had come to see her after Mary had been admitted.

He had told her the maid had divulged the fact that Gary had given Mary the milk and cookies in a vain attempt to make up for the fight that night. But the knowledge of the Fort Yukon letter was a complete surprise. She wondered if Mr. Lasher had written down what she knew they had done to Charlie and Annie and the little store. She had to find that letter. But she had no idea where to start looking! Mary didn't know where it was! She looked down at Mary lying there amidst the white sheets. She looked very pale and very exhausted.

Nadia looked at her watch. The six o'clock dinner was

coming. She could hear the rattle of trays already being served. The candy-striped orderly brought in Mary's meal. She patted Mary on the shoulder. "Eat your dinner now, Mrs. Lattimore. I'll stop in to see you later. I'm glad you have told me this little story. I will have to check it out with Chief Inspector Gregory." She smiled and left the room.

Nadia had no answer for why Mr. Lasher had not come to see his daughter. But, as she reached her office, she made a decision. She picked up the telephone and called Scotland Yard. The telephone rang a couple of rings. She heard the click as the officer on duty picked up the receiver and answered. "Scotland Yard, Chief Inspector Gregory's department. Ramsey speaking. What can I help you with?"

"Chief Inspector Gregory, please." Nadia answered politely.

He came on the line. "Hello, Chief Inspector Gregory here." He said curtly, "Who am I speaking to?" He had been on another line and was not too happy about that conversation.

"This is Dr. Charles. I have just been told of some new evidence in the Lattimore case. I thought you should know, Chief Inspector. I am going over to the Lattimore house to check it out." She paused, waiting for his reaction. She got none. So she went on quickly, "Mary is giving me permission to search her library for a letter her father wrote when her husband and Mr. Lasher were in Alaska years ago. I am hoping he wrote about my foster parents." She stopped, out of breath. Then she went on again. "By the way, her father never came to visit her. Odd, don't you think? Especially when they were so close." She took a small breath before she stopped talking. She waited for him to answer.

"For heaven's sake, Dr. Charles. You must not go there alone! You don't know what Mr. Lattimore will do to you, if he finds you there!" Chief Inspector Gregory was horrified by her boldness and determination. He understood her feelings, but he had to try to stop her. "This is a police matter, Dr. Charles." He was also determined. "You must not get involved! It's too dangerous for you."

Nadia sighed. "I am not afraid, Chief Inspector. I have to do this. I must get proof of their crimes so you can put them away forever." She hated to sound so melodramatic, but she meant every word she said. "I'll call you back later, if I find anything." She hung up.

Then she got up quickly from her desk and grabbed her coat. She caught the elevator and pushed the button to go down. She got off on the second floor and ran down the corridor to Mary's room. She wondered how she was going to ask for the permission that Mary could give her.

Mary looked up as she entered. She knew from the look on her face that Nadia was going to help her find her father's letter. She knew what Nadia came for. Nadia didn't have to ask. Weakly leaning over to her bedside table drawer, she took out some keys.

She handed them to Nadia. "The big key is to the front door." Mary said softly. "Good luck, Dr. Charles." She took a deep breath, looking up at Nadia. "Please, be careful." Nadia took the keys and went out.

She passed Room 209 where her young "AIDS" patient had been. She smiled as she hurried to the elevator. She was glad the new medicine was working. He was an outpatient now.

The cold snow hit her face as she ran across the parking lot to her car. She was very sure her actions would help her now as she drove down the avenue to the Lattimore mansion. She thought about Malcolm's words of danger. But she was not going to let that stop her. If she was in any danger she would always call Joshua. Or, maybe, Malcolm, but she was not sure about that! She did know deep down in her heart she would help Joshua prove that Mary Lattimore was not guilty. The lady just stayed in her mind. She was so vulnerable and so sick! Nadia knew that she needed all the support she could give her. She was so worried about her father and—that lost letter!

She would find that letter!

CHAPTER 12

THE CAPTURE: DECEMBER 1986

The Lattimore Mansion was dark when she drove up and parked at the curb. She didn't want to make too much noise driving up the driveway. So she walked up quickly to the fancy front steps. She noted again how steep they were. She remembered how difficult it had been for Jameson to carry Joshua up them the night of the party. When she got to the top of the steps she found the key and opened the big door.

Nadia went in. The hall was dimly lit. She marveled anew at the beautiful furnishings Mary had. Chippendale chairs and oriental carpets that covered the floor from wall-to wall. She saw a Van Gogh on one of the walls.

Nadia had never seen such wealth in a home. She and Uncle Lazlo had very plain furniture in their home in Nome. But she loved every piece of it. Uncle Lazlo had made the chairs and table just for her because he knew a young lady would like them. Nadia smiled to herself. She looked across the hall to the library doors. She hurried to them and threw them open.

When she saw the beautiful cherry-wood desk and big chair sitting in front of the window with velvet drapes hanging closed, walls lined with books, bindings on them so gorgeous she was hesitant to touch them, she gasped in awe. There was so much beauty in this room it took her breath away for a moment.

She walked across the thick oriental carpet to the desk. She was hoping Gary was not home just then. Everything was quiet! She turned on the desk light. She shivered a bit as she started looking in the drawers one at a time. Nothing! She sat down in the big leather chair, thinking.

She was remembering the much older man who had stuffed the furs in the big fancy car. He acted less flamboyant than the man she knew as Gary Lattimore. He had seemed very nervous and anxious to get away. Mr. Lasher, Mary's father, was that man. Nadia started to think, where would a man like Mr. Lasher hide a letter? She had no idea where to start. She looked around the walls of the library. Of course! In a book! She went over to the first book- shelf on her right. It was at least five feet tall. She reached up as high as she could. That wouldn't work. She couldn't see the titles!

Nadia started walking around the shelves checking titles at eye level. There were so many! She was just about to give up and leave when her eyes caught a title with Alaska in its name. She pulled it out and saw that it was a very old book. The corner was falling off. She opened it and saw Charlie's name on the front page. It was Charlie's old record book from the little store! Nadia would always know it. Her handwriting was there, too. The childish letters and numbers flashed out at her as she turned some of the pages.

And then, it happened! Out fluttered a letter! Mr. Lasher's letter! Nadia was stunned. She reached down and picked it up. It wasn't sealed. She opened it and started to read—It was dated November 1986:

"Dear Mary,

I have written down all the awful events of that day in 1969 in the Yukon Territory. I want you to know that Gary just went mad when he saw all those furs. The old man started to fight with him and he killed the old man along with his wife so we could take the furs. I have kept account of all the sales Gary made. It came to several million dollars over the years.

I am truly sorry for my part in this whole tragic affair. I am hoping that someday after I am gone, this letter will be found and Gary will be caught. Gary has threatened me with death if I tell anyone. I did not want you to marry Gary, not knowing his cruelty and vicious temper.

I planned the theft of money from Joshua's bank so that I could get away from Gary. You found out and took it before I could stop you. Poor Mary! If someone is reading this letter now, I'm dead. I'm so sorry, Mary. I love you, my darling daughter.

Goodbye.

Your Father"

Nadia folded it up, put it back in the envelope and shoved it back into the old book. She turned and started to walk back toward the library doors. Suddenly, there was Gary Lattimore! The semi-automatic handgun was aimed at her stomach. "I'll take that book, Dr. Charles."

He demanded angrily, eyes glassy.

"No. I'm not going to give you anything!" Nadia answered coolly. All the while, she was thinking how she could get away from him. He was between her and the library doors.

"I said, give me that book!" Gary was screaming now. He was waving the semi-automatic gun at her, in fact, dangerously close to her heart. It could go off at any second!

"No." Nadia said again. She noted that he had started to shake uncontrollably. He seemed to have forgotten the semi-automatic gun in his hand. She watched him intently, never moving. She saw that ugly, awful smile come on his face. She remembered a time long ago when she had seen it before. She knew then that Gary Lattimore had lost his reason. He was mad! And he had the semi-automatic gun! She saw it in his hand, hanging down at his side. Nadia didn't know how long he would keep his arm down. She was suddenly afraid!

Gary was talking again. "I killed him, you know. He was going to tell on me!" He was petulant, the glassy eyes looking at her like a little boy who had just ripped up his teddy bear.

Nadia fought down her fear. She had to stay calm. She knew what she had to do. She had to disarm him before he could shoot her. Her voice was calm, quiet, "Give me the gun, Mr. Lattimore. Then I'll give you the book." She reached for the gun in his hand.

"No, no. I'm going to kill you!" He screamed. "You aren't going to get me! His voice came down an octave. "You can't catch me, you know." He sounded just like a little boy, playing a game. His eyes flicked from corner to corner. Nadia could see him trying to find a place to hide. She started to move slowly toward the library doors. Her movement caught his eye. The gun came up at her again. "You can't leave now." He told her. "You have to play with me." She saw again, that awful, ugly grin, the glassy eyes. The book was forgotten. Nadia quickly put the little book in her pocket.

Gary never noticed! He was only a small boy, playing a game, but now he was dangerous and Nadia was trapped. He was still blocking the library doors. She stood still and waited for his next move. It never came!

Malcolm, finger to his mouth, and two policemen were coming in.

Nadia held her breath. Malcolm grabbed Gary by the arms. He quickly dropped the gun and started to cry. He struggled violently. The two policemen had taken over from Malcolm. They were waiting for Malcolm to tell them when to take him out to the Paddy Wagon. Nadia let out her breath when she saw the gun hit the floor. She was still stunned by what had just happened. She realized that Chief Inspector Gregory must have followed her. She just stood quietly getting her breath back to normal.

Malcolm walked over to her and held her in his arms. "Are you all right?" He asked gently. "I was very worried when I heard you say you were coming here. So I came right over."

He released her. "I'm glad I did now. We've been wanting this man for several months." He looked into her gleaming eyes. "Ever since you told us about the Alaska incident."

Gary started to talk when he realized he wasn't going to get loose. Nadia heard him confess to the murder of her foster parents, how he poisoned Mary's milk, and how he had killed Robert Lasher when he was asleep upstairs. He stuck out his chest and declared, out of nowhere, that he and Amelia were in love. "She had my baby!" He started to jump up and down, laughing in glee. "My baby!" The policemen tried to stop him. Gary was so hyper he just kept talking. "Mary didn't know! I didn't tell her! Only Amelia and me! Ha! Ha! Ha!

"Amelia never saw the baby! I had the baby taken away as soon as it was born. I followed her and she never saw me. Ha! Ha! Ha! She was never going to hold it!" He stopped talking. He just looked at Nadia and laughed and laughed all the way out to the Paddy Wagon. The policemen held him, handcuffed tightly.

"Well, that was quite a confession!" Malcolm observed. "What do you think of that, Dr. Charles? Do you know if the last part was true? You never mentioned anything out of the ordinary when you gave me the autopsy results on Mrs. Logan."

Nadia was subdued, knowing she had to answer Malcolm's question. It was difficult to muster up the words. She took a deep breath and told him. "Yes, I did find evidence that Mrs. Logan had just given birth. I didn't tell Joshua. I knew he would have been devastated. And I didn't know how much he knew about his wife's activities. I'm sorry I didn't say anything at that time." Nadia wanted to say more. "I know I'm going to have to tell Joshua now. I'm just not sure how to do it. That awful man is a monster!" She was shaking so hard!

"We will tell him together, tomorrow." Malcolm told her gently. "Don't concern yourself about holding that information back. I will let it pass for now."

It was finally over. All the pain and anger were gone, washed away in the wind when she saw Gary walk out of the library doors. She gave a heavy sigh as she sat down in one of the elegant chairs placed around the cherry-wood desk. She saw Malcolm's quiet smile and smiled back. He walked over to her and put his arms around her again. He held her tight. She was starting to stop the shaking. She felt so secure in his arms! "I'm so glad you came." She said softly, her head brushing against his sleeve.

He pulled her up and they walked hand in hand to the window. The snow was still falling in flat, billowy flakes that covered the garden with white. Here and there the green shoots were peeking out, a harbinger of spring. They watched the snow fall for a while.

Nadia sighed again. She looked up at the tall, handsome man who was holding her. There was a calm assurance about him she had never felt before. She realized she was happy again, but not the happiness she had felt with Josh. That happiness was total—in her mind it was everything she had ever dreamed. For now, she would be content with this man, Malcolm Gregory, who had managed to bring out her hidden feelings.

Malcolm felt some emotion, too, as he held her. It was so comfortable having his arms around her. But he knew it couldn't last. Even though they lived apart, he did have his wife and son to care for. Someday he hoped to have them back in his life. For now, he just took a little pleasure in the moment. He brought his arms slowly away as he sat her back down in the big leather chair.

"We must remember this moment." He said quietly, then "There is work for us to do upstairs." He hesitated. "But I shall always savor this moment with you, Nadia." He smiled gently, patted her shoulder, and started up the stairs.

Nadia understood exactly what Malcolm meant. Never saying a word, she followed him up.

She never forgot that, first and foremost, she was a doctor and up in one of those bedrooms was a dead man. She needed to examine the body, at least, to put Mary Lattimore's mind at rest. She watched Malcolm open each door off the long hallway. For several of the bedrooms, he looked in, then turned to her and shook his head. They got to the last bedroom and as she came up behind him, she saw the body on the floor, blood all around it.

Malcolm went in and looked at it. "It's Robert Lasher." He said coolly. "Dr. Charles, you had better have a look at him, too.

She went in, grimacing a little. She bent over the body, checking for vital signs, hoping she would find some little breathing or movement. There was nothing.

Robert Lasher was definitely dead. She noted that the

rigor mortis had set in. That meant he had been dead for several hours. She finished her examination and stood up. "I've got to get back to the hospital. Mrs. Lattimore was very anxious about her father." Her hand felt the little book in her pocket. "Malcolm, I think you will need this for your case." She handed it to him. She tried not to let him see her tears.

Chief Inspector Gregory took it out of her hand and the letter came out, too. He picked it up and started to read. All of a sudden, he realized what the little book meant to Nadia. He saw the name on the first sheet. He finished reading the letter and folded it up and put it back in the book. "I shall take very good care of this book, Nadia. Please don't worry now." He went on. "I think we have all the evidence we need to convict Gary Lattimore of murder in the first degree."

She was halfway out the door when he came up to her and held her once again. There was admiration shining in his eyes. "You are a remarkable young woman!"

The hug was barely felt, but Nadia smiled happily and said, "Thank you, Malcolm. You have been a marvelous friend, too. I've got to go now. I'll see you in court!" She practically ran down the stairs and out to her car. She was smiling all the way to the hospital.

Chief Inspector Gregory finished his examination of the bedroom, made sure the little book was in his jacket pocket, and followed the paramedics with Robert Lasher's body strapped on the gurney heading for the AID van.

"We'll be taking the body to the morgue, sir." The paramedic driver told him. Malcolm waved them on.

As he walked to his car, the snow was slowly falling and the wind coming up was very cold. Malcolm pulled up his collar. The early evening sounds of the city were wafting around him. London was going home. Work was done. He drove to Scotland Yard, thinking all the way, how wonderful it had been, to hold her. As he parked his car in the snowy driveway, he shook his head and hurried up the stairs to his office.

"Sergeant!" He called as he sat down at his desk. "Come in here. We have a lot of work to do!"

He waited for the Sergeant to come down the hall. It would be a few minutes. He got up and walked over to the window of his third floor office. He stood there, looking out over the broad snow-covered parking lot. His mind was in turmoil!. So many emotions! That wonderful soft touch! The luminous eyes! How could he ever forget? But he must forget! He shrugged his shoulders, heaved a small sigh. He would forget eventually, but now back to work. He walked back to his hard wood chair behind his desk.

Sergeant Ramsey came into the room, looked at Chief Inspector Gregory inquisitively. Then he sat down in the other hard wood chair. He took the file the Chief Inspector handed him.

"Good, you're here, Sergeant," Chief Inspector Gregory said. "I want you to look at this file and tell me what you think."

Sergeant Ramsey opened the file, leafed through the papers, and started to read. The twilight turned to black out the window. Another night had begun.

CHAPTER 13

THE DECISION: NOVEMBER 1986

Back at the hospital Nadia went past the front desk and headed for the "ER." It was chaos! Nurse Jacobs was trying to calm a crying mother about to have a baby, Nurse Abrams stood over a gurney with a young man bandaged all around his body, and Dr. Stives was coming over to help wherever he could. He looked up when Nadia walked over to Nurse Jacobs who was holding the pregnant woman down.

"I'll have to do a prenatal examination now before the baby comes out, Nancy. You hold her still while I see how soon it will be coming." Nadia put her hands on the woman's belly. She could feel the baby moving. The woman started pushing and screaming. Nadia told her to keep pushing harder. As the woman pushed, harder and harder, Nadia saw the baby's head coming out. She reached down to catch it in her hands. The baby girl came out effortlessly. Nadia cut the umbilical cord and gave it a slight pat on its bottom. The baby girl started to cry. The woman was ecstatic when she heard the baby's cry. Nadia handed the baby girl to Nurse Jacobs who cleaned up the baby girl and wrapped her in a lovely little receiving blanket given as a present from the hospital. Then she handed her to her mother who held her close to her heart and lay quietly looking at her. "Now I will have to think of a pretty name for her." She smiled at Nurse Jacobs. She looked down again at her baby and saw that it was asleep.

Nadia moved to the gurney holding the bandaged young man. "What happened, Janet?"She asked Nurse Abrams.

Nurse Abrams answered, "He came in burned all over. He has lost most of his skin in a house fire. The firemen didn't find him soon enough. I bandaged him as soon as I could, but he is bleeding through them now. Nadia walked around the gurney, checking the bandages carefully. "The bandages are going to need changing again." She spoke softly to Janet. (She was remembering the old Shaman who had stayed up all that cold, cold night, teaching her how to wrap the bandages when Joshua needed her to wrap his legs and arm. So long ago)

"Change them now, Janet." She said. Nurse Abrams had done a good job. Nadia told her to have the orderlies take him to his room on the second floor when she was done with the new wrap. There was one open next to her AIDS young man.

She looked up. Dr. Stives was walking towards her. He had two charts in his hand. "I'm glad to see you, Dr. Charles. I have the charts for Tom and Mrs. Lattimore here. Tom is rejecting his medicine. I have started him on another medicine that might help his system stabilize him. "I would like you to check on him later, please."

Nadia nodded, "And Mrs. Lattimore?"

Dr. Stives looked at her with a very serious expression on his face. "I don't think she is improving much. She is waiting for her father. She won't eat or sleep. She just keeps asking for him. What should I do, Dr. Charles?"

"I'll take the charts, Dr. Stives. I'll look in on both of them now." Nadia took the charts. "Don't worry, Dr. Stives." She turned to go out into the corridor. "You go back now and help the nurses with our other injured man."

Dr. Stives walked back to the gurney and started to help Nurse Jacobs and Nurse Abrams remove the soiled bandages from the young man's body. He lay very still. Dr. Stives was very careful to pull the bandages off without hurting the skin.

Nadia hurried down the corridor to Room 2A. The door was open and she looked in. Every machine was working smoothly, but Thomas was sleeping fitfully. He would be all right for the rest of the night, she determined after checking the machine monitoring his heart.

Nadia backed out shutting the door behind her and walked to the elevator. She looked at Mary's chart as she waited for it to come. With a whirr the elevator door opened and she stepped in. She noted that some of Mary's bruises were very severe. She hadn't realized how severe they were! Gary had broken her ribs. She had seen the damage when she pumped out her stomach. Also, her arms were broken in two places so that Nurse Jacobs had to put a cast on up to her shoulders. But the hardest injury to fathom was to her heart and lung. Nadia thought Gary must have punched Mary extremely hard to puncture a lung.

The elevator stopped at the first floor. Nadia stepped out to see Joshua sitting by the front desk. Malcolm must have told him what had happened at the Lattimore mansion. Nurse Abrams was holding the telephone and saying, "I'm sorry, Mr. Logan. Dr. Charles is not in her office at the moment. I'm sure she will be coming in soon. I'll tell her you are waiting in the cafeteria when she checks in." She put down the telephone.

Joshua didn't want to go to the cafeteria. He just said impatiently, "No! I will stay right here until Dr. Charles checks in." He moved his wheelchair over to the chairs placed along the wall of the lobby. He was very agitated.

Nadia walked over to him quietly saying, "Joshua, I'm here now. I was helping out in "ER." It was a busy few hours." She looked at him intently. "What did you want to see me about?" She put her hand gently on his shoulder. "Are you in pain? Are your legs giving you trouble?"

Joshua couldn't stay agitated for long when he heard her soft voice. "I'm just fine, Dr. Charles. I came to see Mary Lattimore." He thought for a moment then looked up at her. "Did you follow up on my plan? I just heard all over the news that her husband tried to kill her. Has he been caught yet? " He hesitated slightly. "I need to talk to her."

Nadia had to think how to answer him. After a short silence, she decided she would tell him everything. "Yes, Joshua. Gary Lattimore has been caught. Chief Inspector Gregory has him downtown in the Tower jail. The Chief Inspector was going to help me tell you what happened earlier today." She was watching Joshua's face. He seemed very surprised! Nadia went on talking as she pushed him down the corridor to Mary Lattimore's room. "I followed through on your plan. I took Mary Lattimore's house key and went to her home. We had been talking about her father. She told me all about her father's participation in my foster parents murder. Gary was the instigator of the whole event. He wanted Charlie's furs. They burned the little store that

Charlie and Annie had owned for many years." She was starting to cry. She put up a hand to brush the tears off her cheeks. " I found Charlie's record book and a letter to Mary from her father."

Nadia had come to Mary's room. "Oh, Joshua, I have to tell all of this to Mary now. It is going to be hard for her to understand. Gary, her husband, has killed her father, too. Robert Lasher's letter said it all."

There was more she had to say, but Nadia hesitated. How could she tell him that Mary had taken his money? How could she tell him about Amelia's baby? Would he even believe it? She would have to tell him about that later.

Mary was lying so still! Nadia went quickly to the side of the bed and bent over to check her. Her eyes opened as Nadia put her hand on the wrist Mary had lying next to her body. "Did you find the letter, Dr. Charles? Did you see my father? Is he coming to see me? " Mary looked at Nadia with bright eyes. The questions were coming fast from her mouth. The pain and uncertainty were glittering in her eyes.

Nadia was calm with her answers. "Yes, Mary, I found the letter. Chief Inspector Gregory has it. It is evidence in a murder. I'm so sorry I have to give you this next information."

Mary was waiting anxiously for Nadia to continue. Nadia went on, "Gary, your husband, has killed your father. He went completely mad. In fact, he tried to kill me, too. Fortunately, Chief Inspector Gregory arrived just in time to stop Gary from doing that, as you can see."

Joshua had been sitting next to the bed, reaching for Mary's hand to hold it. He was absolutely horrified at this news. He felt Mary's hand clench. Then she gave a scream and her body went limp. Her fingers let go of his hand. "Dr. Charles," he cried out. "Something is happening to her!" Joshua pushed himself away from the side of the bed.

Nadia immediately leaned over Mary. She checked her heart and her breathing with her stethoscope. There was very shallow breathing. Her heartbeat was irregular. It was showing a jagged line on the machine. She motioned Joshua to leave the room. "I'll talk to you later, Joshua." She said pointedly.

Joshua pushed himself over to the door, turned around, and went out. He knew Jameson was in the cafeteria so he went down the corridor to the elevator to join him. The cafeteria was on the first floor in the far end of the building. All the way down in the elevator and wheeling himself down another corridor to the cafeteria he thought about what Dr. Charles had just told him. There had been no mention of money. He would have to ask her about that later. Maybe Chief Inspector Gregory could tell him. He pulled into the cafeteria and looked around the room to see where Jameson was sitting. He saw him waiting in the back of the room. Jameson got up and moved to the coffee bar, poured a cup of coffee for Joshua, and put it down in front of him as he rolled up to the table.

Upstairs in Mary's room, Nadia was trying to keep Mary alive. She knew that Mary was having a stroke. The news of her father's death had been devastating. She called for the clamps and put them on Mary's chest. Mary did not respond. Nadia tried three times, putting the clamps down and no response; then suddenly, after the third try, Mary was back breathing normally! Nadia gave a sigh of relief. She was glad to see the line wiggle and beep to show a regular heartbeat.

The orderlies took the machine out of the room. It was always ready to be used elsewhere in the hospital as needed. Usually it was in the middle of the night. Nadia saw that Mary was finally sleeping and knew she would sleep all night now. She would check back tomorrow unless Mary woke up during the night. But now, she needed to talk more with Joshua.

She hurried down to the cafeteria. On the way, she stopped at the front desk and called Chief Inspector Gregory. He was out of his office so she left a message for him to meet her in her office the next afternoon at three pm. It was very urgent. She must speak with him. She was hoping he would understand and call her back with his answer.

In the cafeteria, she saw Joshua sitting with Jameson talking and drinking their cups of coffee. She walked over to the food counter and picked up a tray. She put a sandwich of tuna with whole wheat and a cup of black coffee on it. Then she turned and went over to the table where Joshua and Jameson were sitting. She sat down on the chair Jameson was holding out for her. "Thanks, Jameson," she said and took a bite of the sandwich. She swallowed the bite. Then she took a sip of the hot coffee. She felt better after that sip.

Joshua was fidgeting. "Dr. Charles, What just happened to Mary up there?" He was very agitated.

Nadia told him to calm down. "Mary was in cardiac arrest. I had to take some time to bring her back. She is breathing regularly now as she sleeps. I have Nurse Jacobs monitoring her progress. It will be touch and go for a few hours now, though." She sighed deeply and took another bite of sandwich. She was so tired!

The coffee was gone. She went back to the food counter to pour another one. As she did so, she looked at her watch. It was time to close the food counter. "Beth," she said to the cashier, "Have you counted your drawer for the night?" Beth shook her head yes. "Fine. Put the money in your bag and give it to me. You and the others can leave now. I'll lock up when we leave in a few moments."

Beth did as she was told. She handed the bag of money to Nadia then grabbed up her coat and went out. The other employees followed her. Nadia locked the door after they were all out. She went back to the table. She looked at Joshua as she put the bag of money in the files she was carrying. "Joshua, I think you need to go home now, too. I will see you in my office tomorrow afternoon. I called Chief Inspector Gregory and he will be coming in at three pm. I want him to tell you exactly what transpired at the Lattimore mansion earlier. He can tell you everything you want to know."

Joshua told her he wanted to hear it now, but Nadia was adamant. "No! Josh. As your doctor I want you to go home and get some rest tonight. That is what I am going to do, too." She gave him a stern look that he knew so well! "Now, goodnight."

"Okay, Dr. Charles. I'm going!" Joshua turned the wheelchair around and Jameson took the handles. "Let's get these wheels moving, Jamey." He laughed as Jameson pushed him to the elevator. Just as the doors were opening, Joshua turned to see Nadia push a tendril of hair away from her eyes. How strange! How familiar! Where had he seen that gesture? The doors of the elevator closed. The thought stayed with him all the way down to the limousine in the garage. Jameson put him in the limousine and quickly, smoothly they were out on the road and home to his apartment. His heart had that little twinge all the way!

Nadia turned back down the corridor to her "Inner Sanctum." She unlocked the big door and walked in. The light gave the room an inviting, warm feeling that surrounded her as she sat down at her desk. She put the files down and opened them. The bag of cafeteria money was first to catch her glance. She picked it up and walked over to the wall safe. It was open. She put the moneybag in the safe, shut the door, and locked it.

Nadia went back to her desk and opened the files again. She was apprehensive about Thomas and his reaction to the new medicine. She would check on him in the morning. His file was duly noted and she put it in the basket on the corner of her desk.

Mary Lattimore was another story. Nadia was extremely worried about her condition. Her heart wouldn't stand much more stress. She would see her in the morning, too. Nadia slowly closed the Lattimore file and put it in the corner basket with the others. Nurse Jacobs would file them later when she was through doing her "rounds." She pushed back from her desk and started to get up.

There was a white envelope lying on the desk that she had not seen before. Nadia picked it up and looked at the return address. It was from Alaska. Uncle Lazlo! She quickly tore open the envelope and took out the little square of paper. She could hardly make out the words. Her hand was trembling so much. She started to read:

Dear Starflower, (Uncle Lazlo always called her that.)

I have missed you and so have your dogs. Please come home. The doctor says I have to have help now. You have been gone a long time. We all miss you. Please, come home.

Your Uncle Lazlo

Nadia was surprised and delighted to hear from him! There was never a day gone by that she didn't think about Uncle Lazlo and her dogs. Oh, how she missed her Nefra and Lucky, Pal, Nanuk and Pookie.

It would be wonderful to run and play with them again.

Nadia knew from previous letters that Uncle Lazlo was not well. But, how could she go home right now? The Lattimore trial was coming up. More importantly, her patients needed her! Uncle Lazlo needed her, too!

What should she do? Nadia was torn between staying at London General and going home.

She must talk to Chief Inspector Gregory. He knew her situation and perhaps he could help her make the right decision. Why hadn't she heard from him?

As she was sitting there working it out in her mind, the telephone rang. "Hello. Dr. Charles here." She answered softly.

"Dr. Charles, Malcolm here," came the very welcome voice. "Sorry, I'm so late getting back to you. Just wanted to tell you to expect me tomorrow at three. Goodbye." Chief Inspector Gregory was brisk in his tone, but Nadia didn't mind.

"That will be fine, Malcolm. Goodbye." Nadia put down the telephone. As she was talking to Malcolm a plan came to her. Dr. Stives could take over the administrator's duties. Nurse Jacobs and Nurse Abrams would be of great help to him. They were very dedicated to the caring of the patients. Nurse Jacobs was very efficient at handling the front desk and the telephone calls. London General would survive without her, she was sure.

The hardest part was the thought of leaving Joshua. How would he take the news? Nadia wasn't sure. He had his bank to run and his therapy to do. He was really learning to stand and walk a little now. In a few years, he would give up the wheelchair for good. She was so proud of him!

As Nadia walked to the door, she looked around her "Inner Sanctum." She had enjoyed every minute in here. She would miss it!

But come December in a few weeks and the Christmas season, she would go home to Uncle Lazlo and her dogs. The elevator was coming just as she reached it. As she went down to the garage floor, she decided she would tell her people of her decision in the morning. The tears came down soft on her cheeks as she drove down the snowy road. She saw Scotland Yard all lit up as she passed by. She knew Malcolm was working hard on the Lattimore case. She turned onto the road where her apartment stood and pulled into the curb in front of it. She would miss her little car, too. But she wouldn't need it in Nome.

Nadia ran up the stairs, unlocked the door, and went in. The night was becoming early morning and as she lay trying to sleep, the pictures in her mind were of Nefra, Pookie, Nanuk, Pal, and Lucky. She couldn't wait to see them and hold them close to her. Finally, her eyes closed.

Starflower slept.

Chief Inspector Gregory hung up the telephone after saying goodbye to Nadia. He would be seeing her again and that thought made him nervous. It made him realize how much he had missed her in the last few hours.

He and Sergeant Ramsey spent most of those hours sorting out the evidence from the Lattimore tragedy. There was nothing more difficult than handling a murder. It affected everyone when a family is torn apart by death. He knew that he had to have the events in order for Mary Lattimore to understand all that her husband had done. There was just no right way to explain his madness. It had always been there in his mind even when her father and he were in Alaska. Again, thoughts of Nadia went through his mind.

Chief Inspector Gregory cleared his thoughts of Nadia and picked up his notes. He handed them to Sergeant Ramsey, "I need you to type these notes. Make some sense of them for me."

Sergeant Ramsey reached across his desk and took the notes. He knew what the Chief Inspector wanted. "Sure, Chief Gregory. I'll have them ready for you in an hour or two."

"Thanks, Sergeant." Chief Inspector Gregory said. "Just leave them on my desk. I'll get them in the morning." He paused, "Oh, Sergeant, when you finish, go home to your wife."

"Yes sir, Chief. I'll surely do that!" said Sergeant Ramsey emphatically.

The snow was starting to become a small blizzard as Chief Inspector Gregory drove down the road to his small apartment. There would be a few more hours before the appointment with Dr. Charles. Perhaps he could try to sleep. Better to read a book! He put his car in the garage and went into his front room.

His favorite chair was waiting and he sat down with his thoughts. Nadia Charles, she was a remarkable woman! If only the things in his life were different. He sighed. Deep down in his heart he knew he would never forget her!

But now, he had to get some sleep. What he had to tell her and Joshua Logan tomorrow would be hard to take. There was no way of knowing how his words would be taken.

3:00 pm. Nadia sat at her big cherry-wood desk in her big leather chair. She folded over her hands on the desk and waited. The door of her "Inner Sanctum" opened and in walked Chief Inspector Gregory pushing Joshua ahead of him.

"I met Mr. Logan in the corridor as I came off the elevator. We decided to come in together. Didn't we, Joshua?" The Chief Inspector was gracious in his remarks as he pushed Joshua up to the front of her desk.

"Yes, that's true. I really appreciate the Chief Inspector's help." Joshua replied quietly.

"No thanks necessary. I was glad to help." Chief Inspector Gregory responded as he sat down in the other big leather chair.

They looked at Nadia expectantly. She was the administrator of London General Hospital. "Well, Gentlemen, I think we should start this meeting with Chief Inspector Gregory's explanation of the incidents at the Lattimore mansion two days ago. Malcolm, the floor is yours."

Chief Inspector Gregory was calm in his chair as he started to speak. "I must start at the beginning of this story. Some years ago, twenty years ago, in fact, there had been an illegal fur- smuggling group of men who went to Alaska to steal and pillage the settlements up there.

One of those settlements was a small territory called Fort Yukon. In that group of men were two especially cruel and inhuman men. They found their way to Fort Yukon one afternoon in the winter and came across the little store of a family named Charlie and Annie Moccos. These men stole their furs and when Charlie fought back, one of these men killed him and his wife, Annie. In retribution, this cruel man burned the little store down. Everyone in that small settlement didn't see or hear anything, so the two men got away scot-free.

Then, a few months ago, I happened to go to a party at the Lattimore mansion. At that party I met a beautiful, charming young woman. She and I were talking and I mentioned Alaska in passing. She told me she was familiar with the territory and proceeded to tell me a horrifying story!

That story was about the killing of her foster parents. She was a witness of the murder and the burning of the little store. She gave me the names of the two men she saw. I'm sure you know who these men are. Gary Lattimore and...."

"Robert Lasher!" Joshua chimed in. "I have known these men since my school days"

"I went to school with Mary Lasher. She was a friend of my wife, Amelia. Please go on, Malcolm. Tell us who the witness was." Joshua was getting excited now. He wanted to hear more.

Malcolm did go on, but he kept looking at Nadia. She said nothing, "As you know, Joshua, I was uncomfortable with your plan to involve Dr. Charles. But she was determined to help you search the Lattimore mansion. She wanted to find out who stole your money as much as you did. She did everything you asked her to do. I commend her for that.

When she went to the Lattimore mansion to look for the letter Mrs. Lattimore said her father wrote, I followed her. I knew Gary Lattimore was a dangerous man. You see, I checked the young woman's story with the Alaskan authorities. They told me that her story was very true. They were delighted to find these two men after so many years. Their warrant was still open on them. They needed to know who the witness was. I had to tell them so they could close their files."

Nadia moved in her chair. She made a very imperceptible gesture with her finger to her mouth. She knew he was about to say her name. He couldn't do that now!

Malcolm saw the gesture. "The Alaskan authorities and I have promised to keep this witness under wraps. No one will ever know who it is as long as the Lattimores are alive."

He finished talking and took a deep breath. "Joshua, you were right about the money being taken by the Lattimores. But you had the wrong one. It was Mary who took it out of the vault that day. Her father saw her. When he went to Gary with that news, Gary flew into an insane rage. Robert Lasher made the mistake of telling him he was going to tell me all about the Alaskan murder and fire. Gary went berserk and killed him. Dr. Charles and I found him in an upstairs bedroom. I have his body in the morgue now waiting for the autopsy to be done and Mary Lattimore can make arrangements for his burial. I have also made arrangements for Mary Lattimore to be put in a sanitarium. She will have good care there."

"Malcolm, my bank, Grantwood-Logan, will take over the operations of the Lattimore mansion. In a few days we will close it. Dr. Charles, if there is anything that you want to keep, let me know so that I can give it to you," Joshua said.

Nadia shook her head. "No, Joshua. There was nothing I would want." She had to pause and think before she spoke again. "I have something else to tell you. You must prepare yourself. Be strong! Gary Lattimore is a very cruel and insane man, remember, so what I tell you now, you have to decide for yourself if it's true. Gary screamed at me that he and your wife, Amelia, had a baby. He was very sure in his mind that it was his baby."

Joshua was stunned!

Nadia continued with this devastating news. "I did find evidence that there was a birth when I did her autopsy. It was so little evidence that I didn't really take note of it. Josh, I'm so sorry. Did you know if Amelia was pregnant? Did she ever say anything to you? Was she sick some mornings?"

"No! No! She never let me see her in the mornings. Except once! I remember she was sick when I looked in this one day. Elana shut the door fast when she saw me sitting there. I never thought anymore about it." Joshua put his head down so that Dr. Charles and Malcolm would never see his tears.

Nadia's heart was about to break when she saw Joshua crying. She knew what a caring, sensitive man he was. (So many times he would tell her his thoughts and feelings when he was bundled up in the sled as they were racing across the tundra.)

"I have some more news to tell you, gentlemen. I have received a letter from my Uncle in Nome. He tells me I must come home. Those were his words. He needs my help. His doctor told him he was getting sicker. So I have decided to leave London General Hospital at the end of the week. I am going home."

Nadia stood up and walked around the desk to Malcolm. She took his hand and held it a moment. "I have really enjoyed your expertise and companionship these past few months. Malcolm, you have been a good friend. It was such a short time to know you. I'll miss you so much. I thank you from the bottom of my heart for all you have done for me."

She took her hand away and turned to Joshua. She knelt down in front of the wheelchair. She took his hands in hers gently squeezing them. Joshua kept his head down, but she could see his tears. "Joshua, I want you to continue with your therapy. You have a very successful bank to look after, too. I have heard people say it will be the largest bank in London one day."

Nadia gave his hands another little squeeze. "I don't want to say goodbye, but I must." She got to her feet and looked at her watch. 4:30 pm. It was time to go on her "Rounds." It would be one of the last times she would be doing it.

"Goodbye, Chief Inspector Gregory. Goodbye, Joshua. I'll see you both at the Lattimore trial in a few days. Now I must go." She gave each of them a slight smile and a wave of her hand then walked to the door of her "Inner Sanctum." She opened it and went out into the corridor, shutting the door behind her.

Malcolm looked at Joshua. Joshua looked at Malcolm.

There was so much to say, but they couldn't seem to find the right words to express their feelings. Chief Inspector Gregory started first, "Well, I guess we should be going now, Joshua. I can't do anymore for you until the trial." He got up from the big leather chair and walked over to Joshua who was sitting motionless in his wheelchair. "Do you want me to call for Jameson?"

"No. I can manage for myself. Jameson will be at the elevator waiting for me. I want to thank you for everything, Malcolm. You have really been a godsend to me. I will be at the trial. I want to see Lattimore get what he deserves." He wheeled himself over to the door of the office and the two men went out together. Just the way they had gone in. At the elevator they went their separate ways. It was going to be a trial to end all trials and the people of London would be hanging on every word that the lawyers and Judge would say.

This Christmas season would be the greatest season of the year!

CHAPTER 14

SAYING GOODBYE: DECEMBER 1968

The holiday season was definitely in the air. Everywhere there were hung red and green garlands around lampposts, bright, blinking lights in shop windows, and people hurrying by carrying their packages all wrapped in Christmas paper. The mood was festive. Even Nadia was caught up in it.

The events of the earlier days were past. The Lattimore trial had been carried in all the tabloids for two weeks until, finally, it was finished. Gary Lattimore had been convicted and sentenced. Now he was in jail for the rest of his life. He would not be paroled. The death of Robert Lasher was printed on the back page of the London Times in the obituary column. No mention was made of Mary Lattimore.

But Nadia knew, courtesy of Chief Inspector Gregory, that she had been put in a sanitarium.

She had suffered a stroke after learning of her father's

death. When Joshua told her that the beautiful Lattimore mansion had been taken over by his bank, the Grantwood-Logan bank, she was completely devastated. It took Nadia and Nurse Abrams several hours to calm her.

Nadia felt very sorry for her. She had found Mary to be a soft, quiet girl who never really came out of her shell. Poor Mary! She had never seemed to remember her husband, but she always had her emeralds. She really did love them! The orderlies would put them on her chest every night. Mary would hold them in her good hand. She would stroke them and pet them, never letting them be far from her reach.

One night Nurse Jacobs found her sleeping the sleep of eternal rest. The emeralds lay gleaming in her hand. Nurse Jacobs put them in the velvet-lined box and took them to Nadia who was in her office "the Inner Sanctum. She stared at them as they lay on her desk. Poor Mary! She thought again. The box was open and she put the emeralds back in it. And closed it. They would be all right in her safe for the time being. But she would do that later. She picked up the velvet-lined box and put it in her pocket.

Later that evening Mary's lawyer came to Nadia's office. He laid Charlie's old record book and the fur throw from Mary's sofa on her desk. She took the emeralds out of her pocket and put the little velvet-lined box next to the fur. Mr. Jacks explained that Mary had bequeathed the emeralds to Nadia as a token of atonement.

Nadia understood. She thanked Mr. Jacks and he left. She looked down at her small inheritance. She ran her hand over them tenderly. Suddenly, she could hold back the tears no longer. They came streaming down her cheeks. She put her head down on the fur throw and cried! It was time to go home!

The next day Nadia went shopping for a Christmas present for Uncle Lazlo. She looked at the scarf she was planning to buy for him. He will like the bright colors she thought. When she got back to her apartment, she started to pack.

Everything was going with her, the framed diploma that showed her graduation, the certificate that told the world of her appointment as administrator of London General Hospital. How proud she was of that! All the other little knick-knacks that she had collected over the years, she put in her suitcase one by one, remembering who gave her the china vase with pretty flowers on it, the little dog statue that looked just like Nefra. She felt like she was floating! She was going home! Back to Nome and all the snow! Back to Uncle Lazlo! Back to her beloved dogs!

She knew they were all right because Uncle Lazlo wrote her every month. But his last letter sounded so sad and lonely! She had to tell her employees that she must go home.

Nadia called the meeting to tell her employees of her decision to go home the very next morning. Dr. Stives, Nurse Jacobs, and Nurse Abrams were the first to arrive in her office. The little cashier, Beth, from the cafeteria came next. Her eyes were red from crying. Nurse Jacobs was trying to stay calm, but her eyes were red, too.

"As you probably know," Nadia started out, "I am leaving London General hospital at the end of the week. Dr. Stives will be the new administrator now."

Nancy Jacobs was sad. Dr. Charles had been a good friend. "I'll miss you in the 'Zoo,' Dr. Charles." She walked over to Nadia and hugged her close. "Have a good life wherever you are." She smiled and added, "I've always heard Alaskan food is good for you." The tears were streaming down Nancy's cheeks again, but she was trying to smile.

Nadia squeezed her gently and said softly, "Oh, Nancy, You are such a good friend."

She sighed and gave a small grin. "You're right about the food." She was beginning to choke.

"Goodbye now."

Dr. Stives and Nurse Abrams walked over to Nadia and each said, "Goodbye, Dr. Charles. We have both enjoyed working with you."

Nadia thanked all of them again. Then she walked out of her "Inner Sanctum" for the last time. The elevator was coming and she ran for it. Her tears were falling so fast she could hardly see the button to push for the garage. As she climbed into her car and drove out on to the slushy street, she turned back for one last look at the big building that was London General Hospital. It stood gorgeous in the evening twilight. She knew she would never forget all the years she had spent there.

CHAPTER 15

NOME. CHRISTMAS: DECEMBER 1986

The snow was falling faster now as Starflower put her suitcase by the door. She walked over to look out once more at the streets of London. The traffic was ebbing and flowing on the street below. Shoppers were laughing as they hurried by.

The Christmas music from the Salvation Army bell ringers floated up to her ears. She was remembering her good life here, but now, it was time to go home. She watched a black and shiny limousine go by and thought of Joshua. Why hadn't he remembered her? So strange! Perhaps he will—some day—she would always hope.

And Malcolm—he had been such a delight! Always making her laugh when she was feeling low, always there for a lunch, a walk in the park, and never asking too much from her. It seemed he understood her feelings. She really had appreciated him! But she didn't love him. He sensed this because the last time in the park he told her he was going up to Northhampton to make amends with his estranged wife and son. Being with Nadia had brought him to the realization that he was missing them. He was going to spend this holiday season with them.

She was happy for him. She also knew that feeling of missing someone. "That's marvelous, Malcolm."

He gave her a hug and said quietly, "You're a very beautiful woman, Nadia. I hope your dream comes true." He hesitated, cleared his throat, and looked away for a moment. "I am very fond of you, you know." He kissed her gently, squeezed her hand, and walked away.

She watched him go with tears in her eyes. He was so tall, so proud. She was so fond of him, too. But he was not her lover. She turned and walked back toward her apartment. The evening lights came on as she went out of the park.

Starflower stood a few more moments at the window, looking out over the snow in the street below. She was remembering another snowfall long ago. Her eye caught a movement at the curb. Her taxi was pulling up. She put her key to the apartment down on the table by the door. She grabbed up her suitcase and ran down the flight of stairs. The driver had the door open. She climbed in, and they were on their way to Heathrow Airport. She was so excited she chattered all the way. All she could think of was home.

The cabbie just listened and drove. When they pulled up to the Heathrow Airport curb, she paid him and got out. She carried her suitcase in her hand and ran all the way to the boarding area. She showed her ticket to the stewardess. The stewardess showed her to her seat and put her suitcase in the luggage compartment above her seat. "Fasten your seatbelt, " she said as Starflower sat down. At liftoff, Starflower felt the 737 Lear Jet rise into the air. She sighed a deep sigh. She was going home!

An hour over Canada, they had dinner. Starflower could

hardly taste it. She did eat it and realized it was tasty. She needed all her strength for the rest of the flight. When she finished, she laid her head back against her seat and let the drone of the engines lull her to sleep.

The shaking awakened her. She heard a voice saying, "Please get ready, Miss. We are about to land." The stewardess went down the aisle and sat in her seat at the front right behind the pilot's cabin. Starflower looked out the window and down. She saw lights through the clouds.

The lights of the Nome Airport were just below. They would be on the ground in a few minutes. When she heard the swish of wheels hitting the snow-covered runway, she let her breath out. Nome, at last!

Everyone was filing out and Starflower joined them. They all made their way down the ramp into the main concourse. She found herself surrounded by the other passengers who were finding their families waiting for them. She looked around. She didn't see him at first.

"Starflower." She heard her name. She turned around again and saw him. The big man was standing alone. "My little girl, you are home." He put his big arms around her and squeezed. He still could give her a "Bear Hug." She basked in the warmth of the hug. "Uncle Lazlo! Oh, I'm so glad to be home1"

Uncle Lazlo picked up her suitcase. "Come, we go home now." He said gruffly. He took her arm and propelled her out to the sled and dogs waiting at the curb. Her sled! Her dogs!

There was Lucky and Pal, Nanuk and Pookie, and up front, of course, Nefra. Her big beautiful Nefra twitching her ears, pawing the ground, ready to run. Starflower put her arms around Nefra's neck and hugged. Nefra licked her face. Starflower laughed as she climbed into the sled. She ran her hand over the fur blanket. It was soft and warm and she wrapped it around herself. She felt the cold wind on her face It was exhilarating! She called to him, "I'm ready, Uncle Lazlo." He gave the command to the dogs and off they went, Nefra leading.

Starflower just laughed as Uncle Lazlo talked. He told her jokes and stories about what had happened while she was gone. The sled just kept sliding along. She put her hand up and tried to catch the snow as it fell on her face. She couldn't do it so she stuck out her tongue to catch the snowflakes just like when she was a small girl! Uncle Lazlo laughed then. He was ecstatic! Starflower was home! His life was complete! They would have a fine Christmas now.

It was three days until Christmas. Joshua sat at his desk in the Vancouver Bank. He thought of all the events that had led him here after all these years. The Grantwood-Logan Bank stockholders had heard the news that this bank was about to go under. They realized the bank had meant a lot to his father once so they decided to have the Grantwood-Logan Bank buy it.

That meant the Vancouver Bank would stay open. There was no denying that the people and the city needed it. He wasn't sure just how he felt about this transaction. But he had told the stockholders he would check everything out. He would have to audit the books and meet his new employees. So, here he was! Sitting in his father's old chair at his father's old desk. Now that all the details were taken care of, he was free to go. The bank was closed and his new employees were on their way home to their families carrying the good news of a substantial bonus with them.

The ghosts were all around him as he sat there alone. He saw them—Amelia, laughing and chattering as she ran down the hall—his father, correcting a teller in her cage, as he was always prone to do—and there was Mr. Lasher, so serious, and yet, always willing to take Mary for an ice cream—and there he was, running after Amelia, laughing with her as they walked along—he closed his eyes and shook his head. It was time to go. His mother had planned a lovely dinner for him. Jameson was waiting outside by the limousine. The ghosts would not disappear.

The memories danced around in his head. The snow was white and cold! He could feel it falling against his cheek as the sled sluiced along—the pain was intense. She had bandaged his arm adequately. There was nothing she could do for his legs---he knew that, but the frustration was there anyway. He saw her face looking down at him, her glistening eyes full of compassion.

She had pushed the hood back from her shining, dark hair. The tendrils flowed around her face like heavenly ribbons of spun silk. He could hear her soft crooning as they ran along the hard white snow---he closed his eyes, held his head in his hands. That lovely face! He couldn't forget it! Every time he saw the snow falling he thought of Alaska ---and that face! He was smiling.

The room was beginning to get cold. He should go now. But something held him. His mind still went back----to Galena, those charming people---she was feeding him and they were laughing all the while---suddenly, it came to him. The laughing, the dark glistening eyes so filled with love and compassion, her hug and the whispered "I'm so proud of you, Joshua."

Of course, Nadia! It was Nadia! Always Nadia! She had been there----in therapy, always encouraging him when he thought he couldn't do it---the party, so cool when he had stupidly forgotten her flowers---even in the cafeteria that day he was dedicating the new wing---always she had been there!

How could he have been so blind!

He had always loved Amelia, but there was no answering

love from her when he had needed it. Always, there had been love and understanding from Nadia. His heart pounded with joy. He thought it would burst right out of his skin. He had to tell her he remembered—everything—Nadia/Starflower! He had to find her! He stood up awkwardly. The canes were still cumbersome, but Dr. Stives said it would become easier as he got used to them.

The wheelchair days were over.

He walked out the door, locked it and got into the Limousine that quickly pulled up to the curb. Jameson saw him standing there and knew where they were going. They needed no words as he helped Joshua in. These two were friends, not Boss and employee now, more like two brothers. There was never one without the other. Joshua leaned over and patted Jameson on the shoulder. Jameson grinned.

That night, after dinner, and after Elana had cleared the table, Lucille Logan sat patiently, slowly sipping her coffee. She was waiting for Joshua to speak. Her son had been particularly quiet during the meal. Finally, he looked over at her and, again, admired her. The blue eyes were still magnificent, even in her old age.

"Mother, I have to go. I can't put it off any longer." Joshua got up and went to her side. He stood next to her chair with the canes holding him steady.

"Of course, my dear. I am sure she is waiting for you." Her blue eyes twinkled. She knew the story of his flight and of Starflower, at least as much as he could remember. Now she knew, as she had known all along, he would have to go back to find her.

Joshua held her hand. "Thanks for understanding, Mother." He bent down and kissed her cheek. "I love you for it." He walked slowly out, maneuvering the canes as gracefully as he could. This time he would go alone.

It was the afternoon of Christmas Eve. The air was very

cold and she thought invigorating. Starflower was out on the tundra running her sled and dogs. She noticed Nefra slowing down. The snow had stopped for a while, so she decided to turn back to the cabin. The dogs needed their rest. The sled was sluicing along smoothly when she looked up and saw him on the horizon. Her heart stopped! Was it? It had to be!

She started running toward him. She stopped when she saw the canes as he walked slowly toward her and stopped. He had to catch his breath. It was hard to walk in the snow.

Starflower came up to him and stood still, waiting. The cold Arctic wind was blowing her hair around her head. She put a hand up to hold it. Nefra lay quiet with the other dogs. She seemed to know this man. She gave a soft whine of recognition—Joshua heard it and grinned. He remembered Nefra. But it was Nadia he really was seeing—and yet—that face!

And then, she smiled!

"Starflower, is it you? really you?" Joshua cried eagerly, grabbing her hand in his. He almost fell as the canes came out of his grip. He caught his balance. "I have found you?" Clumsily he laid the white rose in her hand. He had been carrying it all the way from his mother's home on Queen Charlotte Island.

Starflower's eyes filled with tears. She pushed back the hood of her parka in that familiar gesture, and raised the flower to her lips. Her dark eyes gleamed. "Yes, Captain Logan. You have found me." Her heart was ready to burst, she was breathing so hard. "I am Starflower!"

The canes were forgotten. All the waiting, the wondering was finally over. He was here with her and he was standing alone. Joshua put his arms around her and held her tight.

They kissed!

Later that night, after Uncle Lazlo had been told the story and the presents were opened and put away, Joshua built up the fire. He sat with Starflower in his arms, never wanting to let her go. He told her how he had been dreaming of her all these years, that finally, three years ago, he had started to remember little details about Starflower. And then two days ago, he finally realized that his good Dr. Charles was his little Starflower. Then, when he was sure of it, he went to the hospital and found that she was gone. At first, he was devastated. But his mother told him he had to find her. Starflower smiled. Mothers always know!

So he had come! Always hoping she had not forgotten him!

Starflower smiled at that. She loved this man deeply. The bond had never been broken. She put her arms around his neck and kissed him tenderly. "I could never forget you, Joshua. You are my captain, now and forever. I will always love you."

"And I will always love you, my little Starflower of the north." Joshua answered. His heart was finally at peace. He knew he would always be happy in this woman's arms. He would never leave her again. The fire burned brightly as they kissed.

The wind blew little snow devils up the middle of the road. The cold arctic air kept the people of Nome in their little cabins, but a few hardy souls were singing Christmas carols in the little church. The music floated out on the air.

The wedding had been simple, but elegant. The people had gathered in the little church. Uncle Lazlo had worn his most fashionable jacket, trimmed in seal.

Starflower was gorgeous as she walked down the aisle with Uncle Lazlo. Her emeralds were flashing green fire against her throat. Her white velvet suit made her seem like an angel. Her only flower was the white rose blushed with pink.

Joshua was handsome in his Captain's uniform that Jameson had thoughtfully packed. He knew that a tuxedo would be inappropriate in Nome. When Starflower heard Joshua say "I do," she smiled happily. She put out her hand for the ring he put on her finger. Then he smiled as she put the ring on his finger. The minister then said they were man and wife. They kissed and finally it was done. Joshua and Starflower were really married!

Joshua and Starflower sat with Nefra before the big roaring fire and held each other close. Her diamonds twinkled and sparkled in her lap as her head lay on his shoulder. She sighed, content at last. Never, in all the times they had of Christmases growing up, had they ever had such peace and love in their lives as they had this night. The evening snow was beginning to send small flakes down on the cold ground and Starflower realized that she had to look after her dogs.

She looked at the man holding her and said quietly, "Josh, I am going to look after Lucky, Pookie, Nanuk, and Pal. They need to be fed and watered. I'll be back in a few minutes." She got up and walked to the back door of Uncle Lazlo's cabin. "Come on, Nefra. You need to be fed, too."

Joshua smiled at her, "All right, Starflower. I have some calling to do. I should be able to reach my mother on Queen Charlotte Island now." He was worried and disappointed that his mother wasn't able to come to the wedding. But she was ill and couldn't travel just yet.

Starflower knew Joshua was anxious about his mother, too. She was looking forward to meeting her. But now, her dogs were barking all at once. They were letting her know how much they had missed her. She ran to them one at a time. First there was Pookie, straining at his leach. She got a big cup of food and a bottle of water. She put the food in his food dish and the water in his other dish. She petted him, all the while, crooning the little tune she had learned from her mother. Then she gave each of the other dogs their dish of food and water. Lucky was not going to stop barking. So she put on his leach and walked him around to Pal and Nanuk to calm him. Nefra walked with them, her head grazing Starflower's hand. When Lucky had sniffed every one of the dogs, he was ready to stay quietly in his pen. She put Nefra in her pen and she lay there quietly, too.

Starflower was satisfied that everyone was settled for the night so she went back into the kitchen and made some sandwiches and coffee for Josh and herself. She hadn't realized how hungry she was. The kitchen was warm and cozy. She sat at the tiny table with her sandwich and coffee and thought about the events of the day. It was beginning to dawn in her mind just how happy she was to be married to Josh. Her Captain! She had never given up hope that he would find her! And he did! After all these years!

Joshua came in just then. "Oh, good. Coffee and a sandwich! I'm starved." He picked up the sandwich and sat down across from her. "What are you thinking, Starflower?" He took a bite of the sandwich.

"I was just thinking we should go to see how your mother is." She answered lovingly. "I know how much you must have missed her being here. I was also thinking about all that has happened to us over these last few days." She had to ask him about the baby. "How do you feel about the ----?" She couldn't say it.

But Joshua could. "I don't know how I feel about the baby! I am not even sure Lattimore was telling the truth about it. Gary was out of his mind. You know the doctor confirmed that."

Joshua was looking at Starflower anxious to hear what she would say.

"I love you, Josh. I always have. And even though we don't know if or where the baby is, I will always believe that Gary Lattimore wasn't lying at that moment." Starflower got up and walked around the table to Joshua. She put her arms around him and hugged him tightly. "If we ever find the baby and it is yours, I will love it ---and you with all my heart." She stood up and Joshua stood up with her. His arms were around her. "I love you, too, my sweet Starflower. I'm so glad I found you and, as you said, if we find the baby is mine, I will love it, too." He lifted up her mouth and kissed her.

Starflower and Joshua sat back down and finished their sandwiches and coffee. They could hear the people outside caroling in the evening light. Starflower thought about that other Christmas night many years ago. How she missed Charlie and Annie!

There were so many memories!

It started to snow harder. That made it the best Christmas ever, Starflower thought as she lay under the fur blankets next to Joshua. She heard his steady breathing as he slept. It sounded so normal! She had to smile and thank God for his miraculous recovery. He had worked so hard to walk again. And now he had done it! She sighed deeply as she closed her eyes. Always, though, there was a question in the air.

Where was the baby?

As the light snow turned into a blizzard that rattled the windows of the cabin, Starflower turned to her husband and slept, knowing that all the rest of her days would be happy.

It was the best Christmas ever!

EPILOGUE

The airport was bustling. People were rushing to get to their boarding areas. The nurse hurried through the crowd holding the baby tight against her. The little bag hung on her shoulder like it was glued there. When she got to her boarding gate she handed the Steward her ticket and quickly walked down the ramp to her seat. She strapped the baby in the seat next to her and sat down. She was thankful the baby was asleep.

She strapped herself in and pushed the little bag under her seat. She laid her head back and waited for the drone of the engines. When she realized that they were in the air, she went to sleep with her hand on the baby.

After a few hours the sound of crying woke her. She knew the baby was awake and hungry.

The Stewardess came to help her with the baby bringing a bottle of formula and a clean diaper. The nurse took the bottle and fed the baby. She never spoke to the

Stewardess. When the baby finished the bottle, she gave it to the Stewardess and quickly, efficiently, changed the baby and put her back to sleep. It would be a long flight to Switzerland.

The man with the awful, leering smile had given the doctor a lot of money to lie to the woman who had the baby. The doctor told her she had to take the baby to Switzerland to a Children's Home. The nurse didn't want to do it. But the doctor told her she would be fired if she refused. She needed her job, so she told him she would do it. She put her head back on the seat and listened to the hum of the engines as they flew through the sky. The clouds were very gray floating past the window. Somewhere it was raining.

The stewardess finally brought her dinner. She was glad to see it. She never got breakfast or lunch before the flight. The meal was delicious. After she finished, the stewardess cleared everything away. She went back to sleep for a few minutes. The engines' drone soothed her, making her forget the terrible trip she was taking. The baby was sleeping quietly. It would be an hour to Zurich.

When they landed, she grabbed up the baby and the little bag. She hurried out into the early morning light. She hailed a taxi that was waiting at the curb and strapped the baby in the back seat. She gave the driver a fistful of money and told him to take the baby to the Children's Home on the hill. Someone there would take the baby from him.

Then she turned and ran back into the airport. She took the next plane that was going back to London. She never saw the baby again.

The next day the London Times headline read—Plane Crash over South of France—No Survivors.

Printed in the United States
212017BV00001B/3/P

9 780979 907647